SOUL TRUTH

Wendy Pilla-Delcourt

Soul Truth

Rekindling the Fire

The Message, Copyright 1993, 1994, 1995, 1996, 2000, 2001, 2002. Used by permission of NavPress Publishing Group.

Deep River Books
Sisters, Oregon
http://www.deepriverbooks.com

ISBN-10 1-935265-54-7
ISBN-13 9781935265542

Library of Congress: 2010939916

Printed in the USA

Cover design by blackbirdcreative.biz

Contents

Preface

s the pace of life rapidly speeds up, with family life, work, activities, and social pressures, we are often distracted from our inner desires and passions. It is easy to forget that there is more to life than mere responsibility and performance. Much more can be discovered and learned in this life than the skills so narrowly defined to us by the world. The ageless, childlike spirit in all of us can capture realms of possibility to live out the joyful life that burns inside our very souls. We are all called to one glorious hope for the future. We just have to remember that innate curiosity, that passion to pioneer the world, and that fearlessness to take a chance on something we believe in.

The stories within my book take me back to the childlike ways of the heart. Children have a natural way of using their hearts, their imaginations, and their hands to create new ways of living in this world. The most incredible thing about this innateness is that it just happens when one is encouraged to dream, play, create, and discover. We all have the opportunity to choose to find this joy within us, even if we have lost touch with it. We just have to slow down, listen, and be true to who we really are. Living with the unconditional gifts of the human soul recognizes the ageless spirit of your inner child.

Dedication

"When God gives a gift he wraps it in a person!"
WILLIAM LANE

This book is dedicated to my husband, Grant (Delster), and my two precious girls, Hannah (Hanni-bear), and Madison (Madi-kins), the force behind my passion and my courage to persevere! I love you guys the "mostest" and I love you to "infinity and beyond!"

To my mom and dad, Jim and Diana, for always believing in me and praying for me. And to my two big brothers, Grant and Darren, who love their little sis!

To my unfailing friends, who know me by heart and who have always encouraged me to live in my strengths.

To Randy Reese and Rob Loane, for the life changing invitation to join you on an incredible journey to discover what God is up to in my life more deeply. Thank you!

The heart of this book is inspired by one of my greatest adventures: the spirit within young people, the hope they bring to this world, their beautiful stories that need to be told, their creative ideas that need to be navigated, their dreams that need to be lived, their voices that make a difference, their imaginations that know no boundaries, their difficult questions that need to be asked, their unquenchable, contagious curiosities that challenge, their love that transforms, and finally, their character that has the power to revolutionize the culture we live in.

Mostly, thank you to God for every day and the opportunity to live my greatest life. Thank You for the inspiration that is drawn from You, Lord, and for the words that You have given me to share. Thank You for the strength to choose joy and to thrive from Your spirit!

Introduction

*"My failures are my gift to others and
my successes are the gift of others to me."*
-ERWIN RAPHAEL MCMANUS

At the end of our life journey, I believe we all hope to have achieved a life marked with joy and significance. I don't think we realize amongst the hustle and bustle of life that our significance exists in our "being" and that joy is a matter of choice. Often people are chasing the future and dwelling in the past, leaving the precious moments in the middle unnoticed. I have had the privilege of being reminded to live in the moment, as children have been my primary influence during the day for many years. Their stories are the inspiration for this book.

The intention behind writing this book was not because I believed the world needed my insight, by any means. This book has become very personal and very intentional at this time in my life. Its sole purpose arose from a missed opportunity to speak at the graduation of the first class I ever taught as an elementary school teacher. I believe that young people hold the hope for the future and have the gifts within them that will change this world remarkably.

My first teaching job was a kindergarten class at West Point Grey Academy in Vancouver, British Columbia in 1996. What a school and what a team! We often talked about a big celebration when the first class reached graduation day. I pictured seeing the students with their hopes and dreams bursting within them, an enriched educational platform equipping them, and the greatest adventure ahead of them, proudly receiving their diplomas with me smiling in the crowd. Somehow, the day of this anticipated party came and went. A missed party never sits in my conscience very well; just ask my family about how we celebrate birthdays for the whole month.

But, my words to these beautiful young people never left my heart. My hope is for this book to be the words I wanted to share to encourage young people of past, present, and future to see the unique gifts within themselves and to see the value that they bring to this world. I thank every single student I taught for the things they have shown me and for the endless joy they have inspired in me even after they left the classroom.

I believe that if you can carry the spirit of your inner child into old age, a masterful life will be the end result! Don't let daily responsibility and an overrated performance lifestyle snuff out the imagination and the simple joys of life.

Keep the clean, pure soul. Hold onto the magic eyes that see beauty in all things. Know your passionate heart that often believes in the invisible. Enjoy the simple pleasures. Never lose the ability to imagine, to dream, to take a chance, to entertain what may seem impossible, and to learn! Take a hug, give a hug, and share your stuff. You are all gifts to this world and can use your life to change the classroom, the world in which we learn, thrive, and grow. Finally, strive to see the opportunity to live your best life!

I am in my late thirties and this book's journey began a couple of years ago. It has taken me this long to get it on paper because typing was not my best subject in school. I actually have to look at the keys as I type. I am not so sure that practice makes perfect. I am also a stay at home mom that gets to join adventures every day, leaving moments of spare time unpredictable.

Recently, I have recently been awakened to a new appreciation of meaning in my life that seemed so much clearer as a young child than it has as an adult. As an adult, I tend to think too much about everything and often can allow the world to define some of my thoughts. I have even stalled on some intuition with the "paralysis of analysis." With family, work, friends, activities, the pace of life speeding up, and the discipline of my inner life being distracted, it has been easy to forget the truths that are part of my very soul. So, here I am now, paying attention to what God is doing in me and through me. Now I want to take my place in the "show and tell" chair, not the "bring and brag" chair, to share with you some stories from my life of thirty-nine years.

I have always wanted to write a book, because words have the potential to create conversations. Words can also be used to bless people along the journey of life. I am a collector of words. I know that sounds funny, but I just love words and how they can move me. As a young teacher and then as a young mom, I put my passion of writing to work in journals. These journals have provided the framework of the material that I am sharing with you now. Most of the words in my journals marked significant moments that changed me or impacted me somehow. The other words included a collaboration of joyful memories, like my daughter's first word or the day that I got the news that I was pregnant. You know, I always thought that I would never forget these precious times. The truth is that when I went back to read my journals it was amazing how much I had forgotten. I think many of us forget a lot of the precious moments that mark significant times, but I am certain that if you collected words about your life along the way, the joy and meaning from your unique life would be familiar to you once again. I encourage you to try and write a journal of life changing thoughts or events to be a reminder of the beautiful life that happens even when we forget to think about it and reflect on it.

I hope the stories shared among these pages trigger something in you to revisit your inner truths and passions, leading you to lead your greatest life.

Story Time

"When stories nestle in the body, soul comes forth."
DEENA METZGER

magination is one of God's greatest gifts to us. It is like a humungous playground of unlimited exploration and discovery. We can go wherever we wish to go, be whoever we wish to be, and dream dreams that have no limitations. The imagination gives life to fantasy and to the realistic stories in this world. It has the ability to paint life's entire journey in the most brilliant colors. It is amazing how life can play out according to what we choose to pay attention to.

The radiant colors of these pages are all the children and young people, the unspoken heroes at the heart of this book. Their stories have inspired the core of its meaning. I will begin by sharing some of the fantasy stories that engaged my students and I and led us to enjoy much laughter and great conversations together.

At the beginning of a school year, I embark on a few personal traditions with my students. I share stories of my life. We enjoy viewing pictures of the people and the places that mean the most to me. Often an invitation to my home or happy place is a priority because most children cannot envision a teacher outside of the classroom; Some kids actually believe that teachers sleep at the school! This cozy time on the carpet always connected me with the children and opened the door to share our lives together. It is an amazing bond created when values of the heart can be shared in relationships.

Stories have fascinated me through my life. I love books and movies. I also indulge in stories that people tell on road trips, by a campfire, or just when inspired. My dad used to read from the *Reader's Digest's* "The World's Best Fairy Tales" when I was a little girl. He would pull up a snug pillow beside me at bedtime to engage in an adventure with *Ali Baba and the Forty Thieves*. We would burst out laughing with the *Six Sillies*. We cried with the story of *The Red Shoes* and always finished the night with my favorite, *Little One Eye, Little Two Eyes, and Little Three Eyes*. This time was a precious time spent with my dad. This was the time when life slowed, dad relaxed, and our imagination playground opened wide, and we ran in it together with all the characters in the stories. We truly engaged in the inspired folklore that described the very nature of people. I used to think that the Grimm's tales came by their name honestly, and I can't believe I didn't have nightmares after hearing some of the tales. The mysterious part of all these fantasy tales is that we relate to them somehow. The ancient tales of Grimm began in 1803 and I was born in 1970. In other words, we read language that reminds us of the historical ethnic cultures of times passed, portraying how Nations united and how people connected. People have been connecting through stories from the beginning of time.

As a school teacher, I have a wonderfully rich collection of books. I have to admit that most of my books to date are children's stories. I love children's books, as they often use simple and playful ways to share profound truths about life. I like to keep things simple, as they are easier to remember that way. Some books I have enjoyed with my students over the years include the following titles: *The Giving Tree, Good Families Don't, Mary Poppins, Anne of Green Gables, Pollyanna, The Stinky Cheese Man, The Martian Child*, and many more.

I treasure to this day the book titled *The Giving Tree* by Shel

Silverstein, as it is an incredible analogy of a pursuing love symbolic in the tree, possibly how God is with us. This story created a miraculous silence in the classroom as I read it, with the children just staring at the pages as I showed them.

I also carry with me a collection of Robert Munsch tales where the potentially mundane moments of life that we all can relate to are made into silly adventures. Munsch goes as far as to make a story out of getting a little boy named Thomas into a snow suit when this little guy is determined not to wear it. I am sure all of us parents can relate to this experience. The teacher actually wrestles with Thomas in this mission to get him dressed to go outside, and Thomas ends up in her dress and she in the snow suit. Quite a picture!

Boldly, Munsch even invents a story about a "Fart" that lives in a family's home. This Fart is so nasty and life threatening that the entire armed forces need to come to the rescue. I know a few of those stinkers in my world. This reminds me of when I was cleaning my house, not a mundane task by any means, and I went to pick up my husband's jeans and noticed tape on his back pocket. I looked a little closer because it had writing on it. It spelled "danger." Love those kids! Sometimes I feel like calling the armed forces on them.

My students and I also enjoy classics like the story of 1964 titled *Mary Poppins*, the tale of the bottomless carpet bag and the world where everything can be tidied with a snap of your fingers. There are many days that I wish Mary lived next door. Let's face it, it is a jolly holiday with Mary, and it includes singing, sunshine, tea, and adventures. The most amazing part of Mary is that she can say the word "supercalifragilisticexpialidocious" backwards. Kids love to say words backwards. My girls even make code names by stating their names backwards. My eldest daughter Hannah's name doesn't help her much when it comes to code. Anyhow, there is always smiling and laughter when Mary is playing in our imaginations.

Let's look at *Anne of Green Gables*, the Canadian best seller of 1908 with over 50 million copies sold. This heartwarming story is of hope brought to a neglected orphan and the journey of an orphan who transforms into a child of impeccable imagination and bosom friends because someone gave her the opportunity. This book has inspired so many of my students along the way.

This then takes me to the eternally optimistic Pollyanna, a girl who bases her life on the philosophy of gladness. Her motto and legacy influenced those around her to believe that "if you look for the bad in people you will find it!" Our family created the motto to "choose joy" after reading this inspirational story. I think you can tell I like happy endings from the story titles I have chosen so far. Or you could say that I choose the good parts to focus on.

A favorite, *The Stinky Cheese Man's Fairly Stupid Tales*, is where we learn that the reality for the "Ugly Duckling" was that he was just a really Ugly Duck! Now what is he going to do with that? Sometimes we discover that life is not fair, and we just have to learn to think about it differently. Not every hope manifests itself the way we wish it to. Many of my students wanted to dress up as the Ugly Duck after this story was shared. It was amazing to see them challenged to work within the same circumstances as the duck in the story. The Ugly Duck actually became the most important character in our role playing activities. All of a sudden it was incredibly cool to be ugly. It says something about attitude and perspective.

As a little aside, *The Stinky Cheese Man* also has a special place in my heart. It symbolizes a central theme in my life. I was in the intensive care unit at the Vancouver General Hospital after a 14 hour surgery that was deemed unsuccessful. After my dad broke the news to me and decorated my room with singing clowns, peppermint foot cream, and bags of goodies, my mom sat with this book in hand and began to read. Yes, some twenty-three-year-olds still love children's books. There is no better reader than my mom, the most joyful person I know. To make a long story short, we laughed so hard I popped a few staples. Life was good again. It is amazing what laughter through a story can do in scary and painful circumstances.

Further perspective was gained when my mom, who found this time very stressful, went into the hallway to catch her breath. She witnessed a young boy wheeling his wheelchair down the hallway. He inevitably picked up on my mom's state of heart. She stared at the stitches all around his neck and the metal halo holding his head in place. He looked at her boldly and said, "Lady, if the doctors can sew my head back on, whoever is in that room has a pretty solid chance too." My mom gathered her composure and returned to my bedside to share yet another story, but from the hallway this time.

Back to my classroom. A theme evolved that mirrored the moral values from the story of "Pay It Forward." I just used silly puppets to share the story in a slightly different way to the children. Children love puppets and seem to identify with the fantasy but also to find the nugget of truth amidst the play. This story portrays an economic transaction that begins with a gift instead of a loan; what a concept to live by! It is amazing what happens in a community of people when they become "others" centered. It is quite contagious. When children have the opportunity to experience a culture like this they eagerly rise to the occasion.

There were many children in my classes that came from separated homes or had parents that worked overseas for much of the time. It is natural for children to feel the loss or absence of a parent. They would wear their pain out loud and it would manifest itself in different behaviors. I even had a little boy sleep under his desk about mid-day just to have some quiet space. *The Martian Child* is a story that I related to when noticing these out of character behaviors within the group dynamic. There is always a reason for a behavior change in a young person; we just have to take the time to hear them to understand. In *The Martian Child,* the man in the story demonstrates how someone can really "see" another person by not fearing to go to the craziest places to meet them. There is a little boy in the play that acts like a strange Martian to protect himself from any more pain and abandonment in his life. I think we all know someone in these circumstances. Jon, the main character, notices him and enters his world to build a trust and a lifelong friendship with this little Martian Boy.

I see all of us as a little "alienish" in this world today. I know how good it feels when someone "sees" me despite my quirks. It feels so good when someone witnesses our lives and loves us where we are at.

I often ask myself if I am able to "see" people and to love them no matter what they do or how they may make me feel. Being such a relational person, people have an incredible potential to set the tone of my day. I really pray to learn to focus on their untold stories, rather than their actions.

I could go on forever about impacting stories and movies of our culture and time. The very natures of people reside in stories, whether they are fantasy based or true stories. There is a connectedness and a value that is felt that makes the gift of storytelling a wonderful adventure for all of us to embark on. I hope that you will identify with the stories that I tell through this book, as they all relate to the human experience and the journey we are all on to find destiny, joy, and significance. Maybe you will discover some stories of your own that need to be shared too.

I not only feel alive through stories told, but I feel vibrantly alive in the company of people. The people most different from my world fascinate me the most. They draw me in even when I don't really wish to go there.

After growing up in a small town with two amazing older brothers and the most hospitable parents in the world, I decided to choose a career in teaching and coaching. I felt this choice would enable me to hang out with the most people at one time. I also assumed that I would have a huge impact in other's lives. I wanted to change the world by sharing my skills and gifts with all these people! I had big plans.

In my first interview for a teaching position one of the questions I was asked was, "If you could aspire to be like anyone else, who would it be?" My answer was Miss Frizzle from the Magic School Bus. You know, the infamous Miss Frizzle, the coolest teacher ever who travels to the core of adventure and discovery, to the center of experience for the hands-on learning of the very things we dream and wonder about, and the very things we fear because we truly don't understand them. Oh yeah, a day with the Frizzle was like a day in Paradise. I think I had lost the interviewer at this point, but I was really getting into this question. Miss Frizzle always arrives on time, dressed in theme to heighten curiosity, and she begins her day empowering each child by encouraging their ideas to set the course for the day's adventure. She did everything with purpose, passion, vision, teammates, humor, and of course, being a woman, in style! Love her!

I think the interviewer was concerned that I placed so much merit in a cartoon character; hence, I did not get the job. I did however get a job in the field of Mental Health, deinstitutionalizing patients from Riverview Hospital in Vancouver. Really! I actually fit in quite well there and I loved working there! That is another whole book.

After the life changing experiences with the Riverview Community, I finally interviewed for a Kindergarten position at West Point Grey Academy in Vancouver. And so it began.

Who Remembers Their Kindergarten Teacher?

"I'm not young enough to know everything."
OSCAR WILDE

feel the need to write some of my experiences with the lives of young people, because I just love them so much, and I feel like I am closer to heaven around them. "When I was told that I may be asked to go back to my very first Kindergarten class's graduation, and the first class that opened the school was now graduating, I thought, what an honor to be able to speak to these children." I wanted so badly to say something meaningful to them. I wanted to affirm them and to encourage them to live in their strengths. I hoped they would enjoy and have fun with their lives; then this stream of doubt swept over me as I thought for a minute. Would they even remember their Kindergarten teacher? How many of you remember your Kindergarten teacher? Those that said yes get to stay out longer for recess.

Actually, I asked my good friend Linda if she remembered her Kindergarten teacher, expecting affirmation that the chances were slim. She surprised me with a shocking yes. She proceeded to say, "Yes, I remember my Kindergarten teacher very clearly! She was old, grumpy and she made me feel bad." Wow, I thought, harsh thoughts, and I wasn't sure if I wanted to hear more. Linda proceeded to tell me her childhood dream of being a dancer. There happened to be a pair of ballerina Pointe shoes in the costume box in kindergarten. Linda worked her ambitions daily to be the first to the dress-up center so she could put on those ballet shoes and be a dancer. But, to her utter disappointment, her teacher was bold enough to hide the shoes from her to be sure that other children had the opportunity to wear them. There was no point to kindergarten after Linda discovered this news. Let's face it, some people were just not meant to wear those shoes like Linda could! Hmmm…I think I would have wrapped them in a big sparkly box with a humungous bow addressed to the "Dancing Queen" and given it to Linda. I wonder how she would have viewed her kindergarten experience after that?

I certainly do not remember my Kindergarten teacher! This reality dawned on me, and I thought if my students don't remember me, how can I actually have an influence or a value in their lives? Then it clicked; I didn't need them to remember me as this fabulous, life changing, inspiring Mrs. Frizzle, which I hoped to be in my own head. What I needed was for them to know what I learned from them. They needed to know what they boldly showed me every day about love, laughter, learning, sharing, and dreaming. They needed to know the masterful living that they began in kindergarten.

They have made me a better person today as an adult. These young people have set eternal values on my heart. I am reminded always to try and live with the heart of a child, a heart that is curious, open, fruitful, joyous, transparent, and available! Wow! What a purpose these little people have in such a huge, big person world.

My prayer is that as you read this book that you will journey back in your life to that little child and remember what it was like to be there. Embrace that spirit, be reminded of the legacy of faith that begins with children, and the hope that they can bring to the future when we see them.

Let's face it; I know that each one of you has someone you want to say sorry to. I am sure that coloring a picture is tempting on those dark, rainy days. A great family movie in cozy jammies with a huge bowl of popcorn is inviting. You are probably tempted to catch a snow flake on your tongue or to build a snowman once in a while. I am certain you belt out a song even if you are extremely tone deaf. Some of you probably wish to be friends with somebody but don't have the courage to ask. I am sure that you crave a nap or a chocolate cookie with milk every so often. I am certain that you smile when you see a joyful child laughing contagiously. You can't tell me that when a child wraps his or her arms around you after you have been a grumpy bear all day that your heart doesn't melt a little. I am sure you would be sad if you didn't get a cake or a card on your birthday. Finally, you have to admit that when every child asks a million questions because they are so hungry to learn and curious about everything that you might wish they would just stop.

Oh, embrace the curiosity, foster it, remember it, dare to dream, dare to see the best in all things, and hope for the impossible. I believe that is what we are created for. To a child, nothing is unreal, and we all have that child within.

Circle Time

One of my biggest challenges as a teacher was how to set up an environment to engage lifelong learners. I am sure it is the same for people in an office, in the church, or playing on the field. How does one set up an environment that fosters free thinking, identifies unique strengths, and encourages creativity within the arena of standardization and performance outcomes? Tricky!

It is so important for a person to value the learning process and to have input into the journey of discovery in the educational experience. Joy comes from knowing value and worth.

No, I still don't have the answer, but I think it begins when the children are out of their desks and forming circles. In the circle the formality is lost and a different type of posture is engaged. Circle time has a feel of unity and togetherness. There is an intimacy about sitting alongside a friend or a friend that you haven't met yet. It is a relaxed place where everyone can engage in eye contact and feel a part of something bigger. Circle time was a marked favorite event in the daily activities of my classroom.

Some of the best creative moments began during circle time in my classroom. It was a place where each child's individuality could develop through experience, conversation, and body language. This was the place where I could see my students as unique individuals. This was the place where their strengths shone the brightest. This was the place that the depth of their being became the form of the lesson; no lesson plan can contain all of this wonder. It made me think of how much influence this time had in their little lives.

People take all the things they learn from the circles they participate in into the world. The dinner table is the other circle of influence in our world that has a high impact. The conversations at the dinner table play a huge role in a child's self-esteem, attitude, and worth. They take this influence into the places they go. We can often see what is taught in these circles by how children behave in social settings. What a perfect arena to set the course for joyful living.

This was the turning point in my life where I realized that I had to let go of the control of the learning environment and just become a facilitator of ideas through circles of great conversations. I had to notice the unique people who were sitting around the circle and encourage them to become involved. There is an incredible synergy when individuals are valued within a team environment. We are all surrounded by a circle of people in our daily lives.

The problem that remains is that the pressure is always on to perform in the world. There is a lot of tradition and culture built around the performance standards. I guess I just had to figure out what my definition of performance was. A teacher really has to believe in what they teach or it has no value to the learner. I do know that great teaching begins with great questions from teachers and students alike, natural curiosities, and open minds. Brilliant minds come in these small packages; I just needed to have the ears to hear them and the eyes to see them.

Night time, before bed, is a special circle time in my family. The girls get their cozies on and jump on my king-sized bed, along with the dog, the cat, and Mom and Dad. This time often begins with a statement, an unfinished phrase, or a thought. My oldest daughter Hannah may begin this time with a request that we each share something we can work on. Madison, my youngest, enjoys the game "I love you because" where everyone finishes the sentence for each person in the family. We will also talk about the day's highs and lows. Life's deepest mysteries in the eyes of our children get aired on the bed and we begin to make sense of the world together. We thank God for the force behind our family of four and pray that we will thrive in His Spirit. It is amazing how this short but precious time sets the tone of our home and our life as the "Fabulous Four." We realize together that faith really begins at home and grows if we engage in the circles that fuel our passions and personal values.

I often ask myself what types of circles I am involved in. Are these circles developing people or stifling people? We have a choice about how we wish to "be" in the world and we definitely are what we surround ourselves with. Being surrounded by children for much of my life has been a real joy and a real blessing.

What are you surrounded by in your life? What do the circles you run in focus on? How do they make you feel? What impact do these circles have on your life? What can you bring to these circles to lead others to live their greatest life?

Buddy Up

"If you want to go fast go alone, but if you want to go far go together."
MARY AITKIN

he day I lost Andrew was the end of my life as I knew it. There was a huge Children's Festival in Vancouver. The festival was hosted in the Kitsilano Park area. Robert Munsch himself was story telling and Fred Penner was rocking down the house with his silly kid's tunes.   This was the event to see. My students were counting down the days to the Children's Festival. My students and I were known for not spending much time in the classroom because there was so much more outside to offer. Our gang toured all over the city, exploring the mysteries right out our back door. Today was the big day of the Children's Festival.

My Kindie partner Tanya and I were all set to go with our troops to the festival. We had them all numbered, counted, and buddied up. Before we go on any field trip we always review the safety rules. First, everyone is to walk in a line with one teacher leading and the other following. Second, each child is to stay with his or her designated buddy. Third and final, if anyone gets lost, stay put until the teacher or adult supervisor finds you. We arrived at the festival and made our way to the show tent when unbeknownst to me, one of my students, Andrew, had gone to the bathroom. I don't believe we had made a rule for the bathroom. Andrew, being the quiet buddy of the two, just slipped away to one of those big blue portable bathrooms outside the show tent. I proceeded to walk the children into the tent and to seat them in time for the show. After a short while, I noticed I was short one child. I scanned the room, recounted the children and searched high and low through the bleachers. It wasn't a bad dream, it was for real, and I lost a child!

I have never wanted to barf more in my life. The sweat immediately began to drip down my forehead. I alerted my partner Tanya. We began the big search. All the security guards were informed. We blocked every entrance and exit to the fair and then we realized that this is the time when a school uniform was really inconvenient. All the children were wearing them that day, so Andrew would blend in with the crowd. It would have paid off if he had his own style on that day. Then it dawned on me how much children have to go to the bathroom. Often it is a mad dash to get to one before an accident occurs. I rushed to the portables and relentlessly banged on every door for Andrew. "Andrew, are you in there?" I yelled, going door to door. Then I heard this calm sweet voice saying, "I am in this one." I opened the door and there was Andrew. He had realized he left his buddy to get to the bathroom on time. The rule, if you recall from the beginning, was when lost to wait right where you were. Now how many of you would have stayed in a portable outhouse for an extended period of time to be found? Situations can get pretty stinky without a buddy!

I wonder how many times I have left a buddy behind. What kind of buddy have I been to my friends lately? If the teacher chose me for someone's buddy, how would that person feel? Would I be a buddy that made people feel safe? Would I be a buddy they would trust?

One of my favorite stories of all time occurred during my first year teaching kindergarten when I had planned a "Night Lights" field trip to the Vancouver Aquarium to sleep over with forty-five kindergarten students and the Beluga whales.

Our class had a "buddy" that we all shared and even took home for a sleepover on a set rotation schedule. Our buddy's name was Q-Bear and he was a big white bear that cross-dressed, depending on who took him home for the night. Anyway, Q-Bear often began the day with encouraging words to whisper in my ear, or questions that may have been burning within our class but nobody had the courage to ask, a moral lesson for the day, or just an inspirational quote. Word got back to Q-Bear that one of the children in the class would not be attending the sleepover with the whales. Q-Bear conducted further investigation on this matter and soon discovered that this little boy who wasn't going to join us was afraid of something. This little boy was afraid that he would get teased at the sleepover, because he needed to wear a pull-up to sleep at night because he still had accidents once in a while. Q-Bear was very concerned about this little member of our sleepover team that was afraid to attend, so he made a plan.

Q-Bear was particularly off at school a couple of days before the sleepover. He didn't want to join circle time, and he didn't want to whisper any stories or fun ideas to me. He was rather glum. The children proceeded to ask Q-Bear why he was so sad or upset. It took a few minutes for them to coax the problem out of Q-Bear. They all sat utterly dumbfounded with his response as Q-Bear hesitantly whispered to me that he would not be coming to the sleepover. Nobody waited to put up their hands to ask him why; the whole class was verbally expressing concern. Q-Bear proceeded to tell them that he was really embarrassed, but he still needed to wear a pull-up at night just in case…you know!!!

I almost fell off my chair when I witnessed the response of the children in my class. They all started to talk about their issues at night time, including pull-up issues, blankie issues, fear of the dark issues, and much more. It is amazing what happens in a conversation when people get real with one another. Without any thought, all the children agreed that they would all wear pull-ups to the sleepover and that they could even trade because some kids had super hero pull-ups while others had princesses, etc. I was even given reassurance from one boy that he was certain he could find one my size if he looked through his grandpa's cupboard. I laughed and laughed. We all cheered because we were all going to the sleepover, pull-ups and all.

Little did I anticipate that I would have a few concerned parents approaching me afterward expressing their frustration with their child's willingness to regress after years of trying to get them out of pull-ups. Oops, probably not good for my teacher evaluation.

Then I thought to myself, when was the last time I took one for the team? When was the last time I humbled myself so someone else could feel welcome?

It's Your V.I.P. Day

"You're blessed when you are content with just who you are—
no more, no less because that is the moment you find yourselves
proud owners of everything that can't be bought."[1]
PETERSON, EUGENE H., THE MESSAGE

A non-negotiable event of the day in my Kindergarten class was the announcement of the V.I.P for the day. The "very important person" was the class leader for the day and every child eagerly counted down the calendar year to tally the days that they would be the star of the show.

V.I.P is short for "very important person." This title warranted a child the privilege of leading the class if we were transporting ourselves around the school property. This day also marked the day that our buddy, Q-Bear, went home for a sleepover, as well as the day that the child took home the "Mad Science" kit to pick an experiment to teach their classmates the following day. This V.I.P Day also entitled a child to choose the story for the day and to have his or her debut in the "show and tell" chair. I think this pretty much explains why this day is so important.

As a teacher, I believe that the biggest mistake in the majority of classrooms after grade three is the end of "show and tell" time. Maybe some teachers continue with this time, but most don't manage to fit it in. You see, I believe that this is when the real education of life takes place. This is the time that marks new milestones in friendships and provides opportunities for people to share from their lives. It enables community, connection with one another's stories, and learning to speak confidently and to think freely. It is where life reaches the heart level and grabs meaning. It is where children are fully engaged because the stories are personal and very real. It is the marking of healthy relationships.

I had only a couple of rules around the "show and tell" time. First, it was titled "show and tell," and not "bring and brag." It was not a time to show off new toys or to separate the haves and the have not's in the world. It was a time to share stories that told the viewers more about the VIP's life and interests. If the VIP was not telling a story but was sharing an item, he or she was required to conceal the item in something so it was not visible to the curious eye. Then the child needed to come up with two related clues for the show and tell object to spark curiosity. This strategy immediately engages all the children in the experience.

How many of you today have problems with public speaking, where you struggle with words, thoughts, or expressing yourselves clearly? How many of you today have become so private about your life that you are dreadfully alone? How many of you today think that your stories don't matter? How many of you today think about your life and have something to say about it? How many of you today are ever affirmed in your thoughts, passions, dreams, and experiences because you've boldly shared them? I think I may be making my point here about how precious this time is!

Show and tell was not only my favorite day as a child and as an adult, but most of my students shared the same passion. It was a moment in time when it was "all about me!" I could share anything I wanted people to know about me or even to believe in me. It was the day I eagerly marked on my calendar and the day that I wanted to make an impact with my news. I wanted to create excitement, antici-pation, and all kinds of discussion.

I would bring pictures of my family to school and tell stories about our holidays together. I brought my dog Fluffy, bathed, bowed, and prepared to do fancy tricks for the kids. Fluffy gave lots of ambitious cuddles too, which were much needed for some members of the class. I would talk about my dream to become a champion swimmer and all that was going on in my world. I even had the courage to share about the pain of my friend Marissa dying so young in a sand pit that we played in together. The real stuff.

When I began teaching at West Point Grey Academy, show and tell got more exciting than I could ever have imagined. In my class we had show and tell every day. It trumped anything else if we ran short of time or had a change in schedule.

Chloe was in my first Kindergarten class and it was Chloe's big day. She skipped into the classroom with that little crooked smile, cropped blond hair, and big bright eyes, ready for the day. She pro-ceeded to the "throne," not the bathroom, but the special chair of importance to begin her show and tell moment. As she began we heard a racket in the hallway of the school and it was getting louder as it approached our classroom. It was Chloe's mom rolling a rather large suitcase into the classroom, right into the middle of the show and tell circle. The children sat, overwhelmed with curiosity. Chloe proceeded to give the clues as to what awaited our eyes within the suitcase. She said that it was small and could speak poetically. All the children were guessing a recorder, a book, a computer, or a radio, etc. Chloe giggled as everyone miserably failed to identify her item. Chloe moved toward the humungous suitcase and grasped the zip-per, to slowly creep the zipper to the open position. Much to our amazement, a young boy popped out of the suitcase in an Oxford uniform, and with the coolest English accent he began to recite the most beautiful Oxford poetry I have ever heard. Chloe was beaming, just watching and listening to her brilliant young cousin who had just flown across the ocean in time for her show and tell.

Can you imagine such a welcome? Chloe celebrated a person that she found fascinating and she presented him, in his strengths, in front of her entire world. I thought to myself, do I celebrate people in my life that way? Imagine how it would feel to be championed in such a fashion. Way to go, Chloe!

I will never forget the day when a student of mine brought Rosie to school for show and tell. You are probably thinking that Rosie is a pet or a stuffed animal. I bet you would never guess that Rosie is a wart. My student embraced her wart by giving it a name. She believes that if it is apart of you, you might as well find something good to say about it. Later on that evening when my husband and I engaged in our nightly pillow talk we chuckled as I shared this wart story. We took the concept to further consideration. How do we as adults handle our blemishes? Do we have the courage to live out loud despite them? Do we allow them to consume our egos and our attention? Not too soon after my student introduced Rosie to us, Spike the skin tag and Triumhantly the red mark joined her body blemish family. What a kid! What an attitude! Love her!

I had a boy named Mitchell in my Kindergarten class that looked just like the Campbell Soup Kid with the blond, bowl haircut, big cheeks, and a smile that took up his whole face right up to his huge blue eyes. Mitchell wore his entire state of mind out loud. He marched with confidence and a smile on a good day and he hung his chin to his chest on a bad day.

Mitchell's turn for show and tell had arrived. It was a much anticipated day for him. He proudly marched into the class sporting huge, glittering eyes and a smile that spread from ear to ear. He took his place proudly at the throne and began to unfold the mystery of what laid within the bag on his lap. He gave the two clues to the children in the room. He pronounced that the item was silver and it didn't talk. All the kids had their hands in the air, verbalizing the ever so popular, "oh-oh-oh, pick me, pick me." The children guessed a car, a rocket, money, a fork, a spoon, and the list went on. Mitchell just boldly shook his head from left to right as nobody came close to the answer. The shaking of his leg sped up rapidly, and the giggle grew louder. Then his tongue crept out of his mouth and into the corner of his lips and locked in position. His eyes were perfect circles and his hands started shaking as he unzipped the bag on his lap. Obvious moment of greatness!

I am not often surprised by what children bring to the show and tell circle, but I have to give full credit to Mitchell that day, as he surprised the pants off me. He reached in the bag as this funny smell filled the room. He proceeded to pull out this shiny, silver fish from the ice cubes in the bag. The tail came out of the bag, the body came out of the bag, and then there was the blood. The fish had no head, hence the clues, "it's silver and doesn't talk." There were some mild screams and some gross comments, but all in all an impressive response from the crowd. Mitchell then reached into his pocket to pull out a photo of him and his Dad out fishing, having some father and son time. Mitchell was the only one that got a bite fishing that day and he brought it to school to give to me for dinner that night. He said, "Mrs. Delcourt, dinner is on me!"

He gave up the prize for me, his big moment in time; his headless, bloody fish that couldn't talk. I thought, when was the last time I gave my greatest prize away? Thank you Mitchell!

Dr. Seuss is a well known legend of his time and I am sure that almost everyone has heard of *The Grinch* or *Green Eggs and Ham* or *The Places We Will Go*. Seuss has always been part of my children's book collection. His use of language has such a fun rhythm and catchy rhymes that children experience much success with the reading of these stories. He created a very fun and playful way to learn language and to express thoughts. Seuss's material always includes fun stories that often have a significant message for life. One of my favorites is the poem "Happy Birthday to Me." The poem ties right into the concept of the Very Important Person. It goes like this...

"If you'd never been born,
well then what would you be?
You might be a fish!
Or a toad in a tree!
Or worse than all of that…why, you might be a Wasn't;
now a wasn't! A Wasn't has no fun at all.
A Wasn't just isn't.
He just isn't present.
But…you…You ARE You!
And, now isn't that pleasant!"[2]

So children, you are who you are and it is a great thing to be and don't allow anyone to make you think differently or they will have to reckon with Mrs. Delcourt most certainly!

Tutor Your Strengths

*"Be who you are and say what you feel, because
those who mind don't matter and those who matter don't mind."*
SEUSS

believe that educators and parents need to consider the way we understand children and people everywhere. Jennifer Fox wrote, "Strong lives are those that are marked by a sense of purpose, connectedness, resilience, and fulfillment."[3] To foster these principles, we have to be prepared to ask different kinds of questions and to create new conversations. Often, traditional ways of teaching and learning stifle engagement and the possibility for people to take ownership of their learning and to value the journey of discovery. If people don't feel valued in their environment, they lose momentum and purpose, because their part in it becomes insignificant. Significance is birthed from a position of value and worth.

As a teacher and a coach, I tend to love the boundary pushers that courageously voice the questions: "What if you're wrong?" and "What if there is a better way?" You see, the "buy in" has to happen with parenting and teaching, the "hook" that grabs the child's desire so they know why they need to learn what they are learning. A key question I use often with my family is, "What does your life teach?" Does it model your true desires? Does it stand for something you believe in? Does the way we live our lives give freedom to others to live authentically and true to themselves? At the end of the day, we hope that our lives reflect intentionality, purpose, resilience, and joyful fulfillment.

It is amazing how the most humiliating times in our lives can remain a central theme into our adulthood. I had a math phobia at quite a young age when math started to deal with abstract formulas, angles, and letters. Who does math with letters? I needed *Math for Dummies*. This feeling of weakness in me was confirmed by some of my teachers. I think they tried to find the remedy for my weakness within the restrictive teaching style that was repeated unsuccessfully on me for years. Sometimes I felt like my teachers exploited my weakness in this subject, because I think they actually took my inability to understand personally.

I don't mean any of these stories to be examples of disrespect, but they definitely were inspired by a very frustrated student. Math became my cross to carry early on in school. I had one teacher that would explain the process once and then would sit to have a snack while we attempted the lesson. He got very annoyed with the hand in the back going up all the time asking to go over the process again. It got so bad for him that he chose to ignore me and not to help with my processing stagnation problem. I immediately switched to my default mode and pulled on my creative strength. I noticed that when he snacked he enjoyed Twinkies; you know, those yellow cakes with the cream in the middle, shaped like a hot dog. Well I put the pieces together and figured that I could trade favors with him and give him a Twinkie in return for help with my math. Well, this got me as far as the principal's office.

My next go at math warranted me the humiliating name of "Kitty Winkles" every time I raised my hand to ask a question. You can see where this is going. The humiliation was over the top, but by this time I learned to joke out loud to hide how I was feeling on the inside. My feeling of value and significance within this environment was becoming very damaged.

I learned a lot about children when I taught them by just watching and listening to their lives. Once a child is frustrated, it leads to self-esteem problems which often results in children seeking attention in negative ways, kind of like me and the Twinkie incident. Then the cycle of negativity becomes a self-fulfilling prophecy, a label is birthed, and we create a person who is "at risk."

My desire as a teacher and a mom is to change my approach. I want to navigate potential and cultivate the strengths in the children in any environment where I get the privilege to be in their company. An unwarranted boundary imposed on the unique learning style of a child paralyzes them, hindering a child from reaching his or her fullest potential. Imposing methods of learning on a person can change their entire path of discovery and direct them off the trail that leads to their strength based living opportunity.

My mom and dad were convinced that I had the ability to learn these math concepts. They believed that the teachers just didn't know how to teach to my learning style. Love my parents! They were actually smarter than they realize for the generation they came from. When I was younger, I thought they were in denial of my weakness, but now I see that they were both teachers at heart, because they strived to find the way that clicked for me. They also desired to encourage me in my areas of strength so a life of joy and success could be achieved.

Well, my parents decided that they could afford a private tutor to help me with these mind baffling math concepts. My mom invited Bill the tutor to come to our home. Our home was definitely a non-threatening environment, with lots of homemade cookies and comfort. This environment also had the potential to give me the chance to hear these math concepts in a new and fresh manner. We picked a night that worked for my friend Bill to come over and help me with math. The first few lessons went smoothly, and it was amazing how I was completing the questions with Bill cuing my thinking and reminding me of strategies that I could relate to during the process. I was gaining momentum.

As Bill and I got more comfortable in each other's company, Bill proceeded to make these extremely hilarious sounds with his mouth during my lesson. He would purse his lips, gargle and flap his tongue at mock ninety speeds to make the most incredible toilet flushing sound ever! I laughed so hard when he did this. It was truly impressive. Now this was worth learning; this was talent; this was the best part of lesson time ever! I was fascinated by this guy and this sound that my brothers hadn't mastered yet. It was a sound that I could learn and then be the center of gut wrenching laughter. This was the sound to know! I managed to distract Bill from our math mission on to the mission of impossible sounds and from that point on the tutoring went downhill. There was no hope for Wendy…she will even resort to making toilet bowl sounds with her mouth to get out of learning math. I can't say that I am much different to this day. I was okay with math not being my "thing." I have progressed from obnoxious sounds now, however.

As a student and as a young teacher, I have witnessed many cases of children in the hallway, forced to focus because they are just not performing. Or, I have seen the sunken chins of those that don't get to stay in the regular class, because they have to go to a "special" teacher for this block. I have also seen many children get pushed through the system with a red flag beside a certain subject, deemed hopeless. I know because I was one of these kids for math, and I have taught in various institutions during my career. It felt pretty crummy! It wasn't lack of effort on behalf of the institution or program. It was more about a lack of time, resources and options. It can even result in the numbers game. Do we leave the twenty-five that are learning to pour into the three that are not?

When children don't fit into our narrow teaching style box, disapproval from teachers is often the result. In the world of parenting or teaching, we often can take to a personal level their failure to have an ideal response. This disapproval can call for desperate measures in children to find any way to feel successful. I believe that cheating was birthed from this very problem. We often find many children placing all their self worth on how they perform. Scary! As these people lose their true way, they default to become over-achievers, but are driven primarily from a place of weakness rather than from their true strengths. Because they have talent, they can pull this off for a while. It can seem like these performance based children are truly living their dreams until one day they snap. When we cap a child's uniqueness, because we may fear their strengths, we end up exploiting their weaknesses and may kill the very journey that a child is created to live. This is why I thank God that He is bigger than all of us.

I realize now that my parents had it right for the most part. They would often say that the teachers aren't teaching you the way that you learn, because everyone can learn. They would proceed to say that you are so good at this, so let's focus on what you are good at. That statement is more brilliant to me today than it ever was then. As I learned to focus on my strengths, my weaknesses improved as well.

As a teacher and parent, exposing the children in my life to only the things that are true to my desires and my interests is only half of a relationship. When children contribute to the dialogue and get the privilege of personally investing in the topics to learn, a healthy relationship begins, where growth and insight are fostered.

Let's face it; it's true. We can't all be brilliant at everything, but all of us can be exceptional at a few things. How do we know what these things are?

They begin where your passion is. They begin where it comes naturally and where your strengths stand out uniquely. Your strengths are the gifts that are a part of your nature, of your eternal being, that make you feel totally fulfilled. The strengths that are uniquely yours are the ones that mark the world, that start a conversation, that will change a culture, and create a future. The challenge is for someone to notice them, to draw them out, to foster them, and to celebrate them. I often ask, how many times as a teacher might I have missed someone's gift?

Do I see the strengths in the people around me? Do I want to see them? Do I envy them or celebrate them?

There is no "one way" to a future and to a rich, fulfilling life. We can't believe that our methods and styles are the ticket for every child to find their true strengths. I believe that schools, homes, and communities need to encourage insight, foster imagination and exploration, and risk changing the way we learn and do things. We need to create environments where it is safe to ask the tough questions and safe to experiment with new ideas. We either discover if it works or if it doesn't. An open forum to celebrate the uniqueness within one another is essential to reaching our fullest potential and to keeping the ageless spirit of the child thriving. Let's face it; individuality is contrary to standardization. Weakness derives its meaning from strengths spiraling out of control, because the true somebody is not "seen." This just rattles my universe, and I hope that we can move in this direction globally. I think it was Gandhi that said, "Be the change you wish to see in the world."

Can you imagine if the school system and family life at home fostered the practice of tutoring strengths? Can you imagine if those circles focused on every person's potential to grow from good to great? What a classroom it would be, a classroom that I myself would want to be a part of.

As an adult, adapting to change, new ideas, new cultures, and more, I still revisit my strengths. I try to build on them to use my life in a way that is freeing and joyful, rather than frustrating and joyless.

Don't get me wrong; I can poke fun at this system a little because I am a teacher, but at times I think we fail to realize that education, in itself, is a tool to help us all discover our strengths. It is a tool that can pull out the unique potential that resides within all of us. We learn about time management. We learn about dynamics of relationships in the playground. We learn to fake our way through the things that don't interest us. We too often learn that grades matter more than who we are. A teacher cannot teach a child anything. A teacher can empower a child to love to learn, grow, change, adapt, and to navigate a meaningful purpose within their unique lives. The ultimate impact of a teacher is to truly believe in the worth of every soul. Teachers need to model lifelong learning themselves. I know many teachers like this and they are incredible ambassadors of education.

Real education happens in the playground or on the bus. Yes, in the world of relationships. The sad part about learning institutions is that often the tools left to our disposal become the standard in which to live. There is often an ultimate desire to perform within the set criteria. The "A" becomes the ultimate goal, and there is no letter grade "H" for heart. You see, when we begin to live a life within the boundaries placed upon us, we start to become like everyone else. We limit our full potential to leave our own special mark in the world.

I believe the world ultimately wishes to understand all things; therefore, it creates systems, programs, and theories to make sense of it. These established theories and assumptions erase hope and the concept of faith. We then forget the childlike boldness and curiosity within our souls; that very spirit that believes in the unseen and the presence of a power that unites us all. The programs, systems, and theories serve to help us understand so we feel safe. There is some safety when there are parameters and measurable terms to exist within, but where does the journey begin to move into the unknown, the chance, the dream, or the vision? This is when the true measure of significance begins.

I have spent many years working with the special needs community, the community that turns the criteria completely upside down. I will never forget waiting on the field at school for the children to be dismissed. I overheard some moms talking about the recent report cards that were distributed. They were going on about how their children got almost straight "A's". The areas that don't really count, like Physical Education, were where they got their "B's." I chuckled for a moment, because if I recall correctly, Physical Education was one of my only "A's". Anyway, I looked over to this Mom who had a child with special needs. She, after overhearing these other women, turned to her friend and said, "Marks A's, B's, C's, try wearing the mark that my child has to wear." An "A" in school is the big mission for many of these children's parents. What about being chosen for a friend? What about being picked to play a game? What about being invited to a birthday party? What about being noticed on the good days and not the days of uncontrollable outbursts? It was like she was screaming, "What about my child?"

My heart broke for that mom that day. The criteria in her world is one we are all too unfamiliar with. It is a world where your popularity means nothing. It is a world where grades are a foreign language. It is a world where beating someone else means nothing; a world where standards are different. The world that I have experienced working with special needs children is a world where love is the criteria and it is as simple as that!

What criterion defines your life? What are your non-negotiable standards that you wish to live by? Do you know your strengths? Are you living in them? How are you building into your natural self? What makes you feel most alive and fuels your tank?

"Children Learn What They Live"

If a child lives with criticism,
He learns to condemn.
If a child lives with hostility,
He learns to fight.
If a child lives with ridicule,
He learns to be shy.
If a child lives with shame,
He learns to feel guilty.
If a child lives with tolerance,
He learns to be patient.
If a child lives with encouragement,
He learns confidence.
If a child lives with praise,
He learns to appreciate.
If a child lives with fairness,
He learns justice.
If a child lives with security,
He learns to have faith.
If a child lives with approval,
He learns to like himself.
If a child lives with acceptance and friendship,
He learns to find love in the world.

AUTHOR UNKNOWN

Dream Kaleidoscopes

"May your accomplishments align with your dreams."
HECTOR CARDENAS GASTELUM

love kaleidoscopes, because every time you take a close look at the complex patterns within the scope you can see images of constantly changing colors and shapes. The patterns look a lot like broken glass, but they produce mirror images in unique designs that mesmerize and keep us engaged. Every twist and turn of the scope creates a new image and design that captures the eye.

Dreams are much like kaleidoscopes. The scope and sequence of them change as we journey through life. The designs capture reflections of our hearts' desires and our innate soul cravings. No matter how or what we dream, they are unique every time to our personal nature.

The ability to dream trumps the word boredom in our household. To say "I am bored" is considered swearing! When I think about the capacity to dream, I get so excited, because it is both economical and has no boundaries. I can be who I wish to be, go where I wish to go, and accomplish absolutely anything. What an inspirational gift to be given. I think most of us hardly consider the beauty of dreaming. I am wired as a "dreamer," as I have been told many times. I am constantly dreaming. I began as a young girl, dreaming of magical lands, fairies, and talking animals. In my early teens I dreamt of becoming an Olympic swimmer but one that only had to swim one or two lengths of freestyle and nothing else. I love to create in many different ways. I dream of planning many fun and adventurous parties and events that bring people together to enjoy each other and laugh. I've always dreamed of writing a book. I dream of having friends in every country that I can visit and then have them visit me through my lifetime. I dream of people realizing their potential and chasing after it with a vengeance. I dream of the underdog winning and the victim surviving to know justice. I dream of transformed lives. I dream of silly, fun things like doing voice animation for a cartoon character. I dream of riding whales and pet tigers. I dream of my house getting magically cleaned in a blink of the eye. As a mom, I constantly dream of my family being an unstoppable force that can impact the world. I dream of holding my husband's hand after sixty years of being married, still eager to hear him and love him. I dream of driving a hot pink convertible at eighty with my car packed with grandchildren. The list goes on…

We naturally dream. Often, we may not realize that we do, because our thoughts can take on many directions. Images are constantly changing in our minds. Thought patterns are continuously adapting as we experience life. These adapting patterns are much like a kaleidoscope. The cool thing about our dream kaleidoscope, if we look at dreaming this way, is the broken mirror images in the scope. These images in the scope reflect who we uniquely are. They are unique and beautiful designs that capture the eyes of the world as we change and move within the scope and sequence of our journeys.

In my experience, it seems that children have a much better grasp on the whole dreaming thing. They seem to be able to switch from reality to a dream in an instant without thought or hesitation. I will never forget Tanner, a little boy I taught in Kindergarten. He could sure dream. At times Tanner's dream world was inconvenient for others. Somehow, I learned to appreciate it over the years. Tanner had a very limited palate and felt that the world really needed to narrow down the food chain. He told me that when he grew up he would open a chain of restaurants called Orange. The menu would contain macaroni and cheese, string cheese, cheese pizza, cheese dogs, and cheese everything. He was going to have orange dishes, walls, and tables. Brilliant! I bet if he ever does do that it will be the beginning of a rainbow of colored restaurants. Tanner eventually took a liking to green peas. Perhaps peas could be the first thing on the menu for the Green restaurant.

As an adult, I realize that many of my dreams were just that, dreams. A lot of my dreams didn't come true. Some of my dreams were never mine to come true. Some would have evoked much suffering on others. That is okay and how it should be. We can't possibly expect every dream to happen in this lifetime. I haven't told many people that I was literally born a "head banger." I used to bang my head into my pillow at night to get myself to sleep. You would think that this head banging might be cause for concern from my parent's perspective. Instead of psychoanalyzing it all and trying to diagnose my sleeping pattern, I just decided that it meant I was born to be a wild child. A head banger, rocker girl sounded like a great future for me. Not! I sure did a lot of singing and dancing around my house with the tunes cranked up, though. It is okay to have fun with your dreams. I don't think it is a good idea to ever stop dreaming. There is definitely something to be said about going to the place of impossibility and living it out in our dreams. You never know when one dream may become a reality.

I also discovered that some of my dreams didn't take the shape or design that I anticipated. Unexpected twists and turns along the path made some of my dreams even more beautiful than I imagined. I guess you could say it is one's perspective that is the key in these instances.

When I was ten, I lived in the small Kootenay town of Castlegar,

British Columbia. I enjoyed life amidst the fresh water lakes, mountains, and glaciers. My mom didn't know what to do with me that summer. Both my brothers were getting to an age where I would cramp their style to tag along. My brothers are three and six years older than me. Because I loved the water, my mom decided that putting me in swim club was a good start. There were a lot of neighborhood kids joining swimming, and it was a healthy choice. So I packed my bag, got on my hand-me-down bike, and I rode up the street to the old Bob Branson twenty-five yard outdoor pool on the corner by the railroad tracks. There were kids stretching out on their towels under the sun. They all looked like pros. The coach was putting in the lane ropes. He walked over and said, "You're the new kid, you're in this lane." I proceeded to the lane and got in with my group to begin the practice. We were told to swim a two hundred yard warm up before our first set. I quickly learned which side of the lane to swim on. I also learned that going last was probably best to start. I managed my eight lengths of front crawl. I was standing with my group, waiting for the next set to be given to us, when the coach made eye contact with me. "Where did you learn how to swim?' he asked. I told him that I took Red Cross lessons and basically swam in creeks and lakes with my brothers. He laughed and said, "I have never seen a style quite like yours. Did you know that your elbow should not be the first thing to enter the water when you are swimming the front crawl?" I just stared at him awkwardly. He told me my future probably wasn't in swimming.

I was a little off after our conversation and was rendered speechless, which doesn't happen to me very often, believe me! I swam out the remainder of the practice and went home frustrated.

After I processed it a little longer, I schemed that the best way to protest this ruthless, defeating, and heartless coach was to become excellent. To make a long story short, three coaches later I became the Provincial record holder for the fifty meter freestyle. This time qualified for the 1988 National Championships in Calgary, Alberta. I actually still have that record, twenty-three years later. I feel the urge to boast about that record since I had no future in swimming. The sad part is sometimes people believe what others say and they just give up. It is a reminder of how powerful words can be.

Speaking of dreams that take interesting turns, are you familiar with the phrase, "No pain, no gain?" That phrase was repeated to me many times as a young athlete. The problem with that phrase was I couldn't distinguish between a healthy pain and an unhealthy pain. As I reached my early to mid-teens, pain began to affect my performance and my life. This pain, now known to be unhealthy, started to change my direction and my dreams.

From the age of twelve, I spent many years in the hospital, and after many surgeries I was proven to be a rare anomaly. Brilliant, aren't we all anomalies? No, really, I apparently had a vascular anomaly where my body had decided that it needed to grow a third circulatory system. I knew there was a reason I loved the song "Hot Blooded" by Foreigner. Love those 80's! Anyway, the system itself was not the main problem. It was where these blood vessels grew that was the problem. They were growing in my central nervous system, mainly within the sciatic nerve. Unsuccessfully trying to remove this massive growth risked the function of the main nervous system that operated my body as a whole. The other problem was a mutated gene in my body that kept telling my system to grow this mass even if some of it was removed. The by-product of such a syndrome was chronic pain and the loss of muscular control in my right leg. Not the best recipe for an Olympic swimmer's future. No, my life was taking an interesting turn and the scope was changing.

While undergoing multiple examinations in hospitals to discover my problem, I had the opportunity to witness some life changing stories within the hospital walls. Little did I realize at the time that these stories would change my life forever.

Going through all that time in hospitals, my biggest fear and disappointment was that I would be defined by my limitations and potentially miss the life I was born to live. Funny how I could actually think that I would miss the life I was born to live. There was definitely a little drama queen in me back then. I don't think I considered at the time that maybe there was a better life to be lived, even with my circumstances. The definition of significant living was unclear at this point in my life.

After years in and out of surgery and genetic exploration, I pursued a career in coaching swimming and in teaching. I completed a Human Kinetics Degree and a Bachelor of Education Degree at the University of British Columbia. I spent ten years coaching speed swimming, as I still felt at home in a pool environment. The special thing about these times was that I got to see many children reach their personal bests. I coached many underdogs to a place on the Provincial Relay Team. I witnessed a few of my older swimmers get recruited to high performance clubs and get University scholarships. I began to realize that it felt good to be a part of another's success. Being a cheerleader and coach is part of winning the medal.

Among the most precious of my memories coaching was my time working with the Special Olympic Swim Team. It had to be one of the most fulfilling journeys of my life. Spending time with these athletes was incredibly empowering. For every minute I gave, I felt that I received ten times as much back in appreciation. Talk about a great investment return. The whole time I coached, not one athlete turned up late for practice. Not one complaint was aired between sets. I was never short of a hug or cheer when the workout was completed. There was no chance in the world for me to avoid the feeling of being drenched in waves of joy when working with these athletes.

I recall trying to tell the athletes a little about my life. I told them that I used to race in swimming, that I went to UBC and had been a trainer for quite some time. Their enthusiasm began to fade until one of the athletes just came up and gave me the biggest hug and said, "Thank you for being our coach, we love you." The only letters beside my name required for this position were love, not B.H.K or B.Ed.!

I took my Special Olympics team to their first competition at St.

Andrews on Vancouver Island. It was like arriving at Disneyland when we got there. The athletes cheered and grabbed their bags to get off the bus and on with the show. We were all stretching by the poolside minutes after we arrived. There were continuous interruptions of meeting new friends on the deck. Then the moment came when the swimmers could get their feet wet. They warmed up like they were attending the Olympic Games. This was serious stuff! Once the heats started, our team assembled in our designated section. Our cheering voices were on. We sat in eager anticipation of the day's outcomes. We, along with all attendees, yelled and screamed as each swimmer dove in to begin their race. It was amazing to see all the splashes. The odd time after a swimmer surfaced he or she would cross under the lane rope into another lane by accident. Regardless of the journey between the walls, each athlete came home to a roaring finish. A simultaneous victory jump off the bottom and a fist in the air accompanied every finish. This kind of excitement and energy called for the coaches to jump in for the victory dance too!

I learned what winning really meant during this time of my life. I am so thankful to my team for the privilege of joining the road to victory with them. It was all about finishing strong! First place seemed trivial.

Then there are those playful and adventurous dreams that we hope happen in our lives. I have learned that sometimes it takes a non-negotiable act of perseverance to get that dream to happen.

A couple of summers ago my family and I were vacationing in Victoria, BC. Victoria is one of the most beautiful cities in the world. We booked our whale watching tour on the ocean Zodiac to begin our day's adventures. We also booked our horse-drawn carriage for sunset. The sunset in the harbor is a must see for us romantic types. For the in-between time, we were very excited to watch the street entertainment in the harbor. We were also heading to see baby pot-bellied pigs born at Beacon Hill Park. We were hoping that one of the pigs might even accompany us home. What we didn't plan for was one of the greatest adventures we ever experienced as a family.

We left Beacon Hill Park, disappointed that one of the little pigs couldn't come home to live with us and drove to the coast line of Dallas Road. Immediately, brilliant colors dancing in the sky caught our curiosity. There were a number of paragliding kites riding the winds along the coastline. The kites looked like graceful gazelles prancing in the sky. I was completely taken by the energy and the masterful skill required to direct these kites. I asked Grant to pull the van over. I opened the door, darted out, and started running under the kites. I was just ecstatic about the idea of flying like that. I managed to catch the eye of one man, and I put my hand in the air toward him. He maneuvered his kite to my level to give me a high five, and then he caught the next gust of wind and sailed off. I couldn't believe that he could control his glider that way. He maneuvered gracefully amidst the unpredictable winds and the big ocean in front of him. I got my camera out and started snapping photo after photo, chasing these guys all over the place. I am sure they thought I was a little out there.

Claudio, my high five guy, began his descent from the sky a few feet away from where I was running. I dashed over and didn't even say "hi." I just asked if he did tandem riding. He smiled at me. He spoke with his buddies for a few moments and then said, "It is your lucky day, I will take your whole family for a glide if you would like." I was jumping up and down and accidentally jumped right on him. I imagine that was a bit invasive for him! No waivers, no down payment, just an invitation to fly. Are you kidding me? I loved this guy!

Claudio and his flying buddy began to strap in my youngest daughter Madison. At that time, my oldest daughter Hannah spoke up and said, "Mom, you tell us not to talk to strangers, but you will send us flying into the sky with one with no strings attached?" I looked at her and I laughed and said, "Are you willing to take the risk?" She replied, "I am going next and I will take the photos of Madison while she is flying." Madison launched to great heights and had her arms spread out like wings. Her hair blew in the wind and she wore a smile that could only describe the greatest sense of freedom she had ever known.

Hannah went next, while she bit slightly on her lower lip. With responsible anticipation but no turning back, up she went to the level of the setting sun. Claudio and Hannah began to swing like a pendulum with the motion of the wind blowing against the coast line. She laughed and screamed into the wind. She looked down to be sure that we were watching. I just kept on running along the coast jumping and waving and laughing like a mad woman.

Then it was my turn, a dream ready to be lived right before my eyes. I couldn't jump in the straps fast enough. Claudio and I ran toward the edge of the cliff to catch the next swoosh of wind to carry us up. We entered the silence. We rose to the place where a different dimension began. We were alone with the brilliant colors of sunset. The wind blew in our faces while the waves pounded the shore below. The joy I felt was indescribable. Then Claudio said to me, "I could fly all day with you, as you put the wind in the sails." Just after he said that a huge gust of wind grasped our glider. It was known to blow like this once or twice a year. It was said to be the glider's Utopia if the wind could carry you over the point of the bay where the cruise ships came in. It was our day to feel the glider's Utopia. Claudio told me to hang on and we took off. Now I really knew what it felt like to ride the wind. To add to my adventure, Claudio spotted a couple dining on their deck in a high apartment building. He maneuvered the glider toward them and hovered close to the deck. The couple looked up dumbfounded as we cheered them from the sky. I was so giddy, I could hardly breathe. He took me over to see the cruise ships and the parliament buildings and beyond, for the flight of my life. I felt like God himself gave me wings that day. Incredible, I thought, to be able to experience a glimpse of the beauty that goes so unnoticed in our fast-paced lives. I thought for a moment about how little I look up during the day. What a gift and what a dream come true; I just had to chase after it, literally!

The one aspect of dreaming that I find important to learn early in life is the difference between a healthy dream and an allusion. Did I say allusion or delusion? I have heard way too many stories of people quitting on life and gaining a perspective of hopelessness, because they didn't get "the dream" or the outcome wasn't as good as they'd anticipated. We can tend to base our understanding on feelings versus reality. Feelings change moment to moment and can really distract us from the reality we need to embrace. Life is filled with a spectrum of feeling. We need to consider the outcome of how we respond to life. It is really about perspective and choices. It may be possible that one day you could get fired from your job, which could lead to devastation on many levels. Do we ever consider that it could lead to a better job or a better future? Is it possible that we could be disabled in one skill area but can become the master of another? Is it possible that one devastating accident in your life could lead to you preventing the same in other's lives by sharing your story? Do we ever think that the place we feel the most pain in life could be the place we find our purpose? I believe that when God said he uses all things for good, he meant it. We just have to choose to see the good regardless of how we feel.

There is no limit to what you dream, how you dream, and where you go in your dreams. Just dream and let God surprise you with how they play out. You will be pleasantly surprised. If we are willing to adjust our perspective to notice the incredible images, the colors, and the shapes that unfold from our journey, we will see our dreams before our eyes. Dreams, beautiful and unique to you and to the world around us, happen every day. I encourage you to create a dream kaleidoscope way of living. Don't be disappointed if or when things don't turn out how you think they should. The scope and sequence may change in order to make the most important dreams the brightest. I believe our dreams align with our accomplishments, because we have the choice to live with a spirit of passion, joy, and hope.

I wonder how often we talk about our dreams and hopes. I encourage all of you to dream like you did as a child and to recapture the realms of possibility in your own life. Take a chance. Believe in the impossible. Dream big!

Crosses on the Road

*"The place God calls you to is the place where
your deep gladness and the world's deep hunger meet."*
FREDERICK BUECHNER

hen I reflect on images that have impacted me profoundly since I was a little girl I see crosses on the road, the crosses that randomly come as we pass so quickly heading to and fro in our lives. Many of them are decorated with flowers, pictures, and sometimes words. I often feel like stopping at the crosses to notice the lives that have ended here on the journey. I always well up when I pass crosses on the road because they make me feel a little surreal. Sadness prevails, wondering if all these people, marked by a cross, were noticed in their life. How much time did they get? Did they get to live their dreams? Did they get to see the beauty that this life brings? Where did they go? All these questions randomly run through my thoughts as I quietly pass the crosses.

Death became real to me for the first time when my friend Marissa, at the age of ten, died in a sand pit that we played in as children. We were playing in a cave dug in the sand one day, and the next she was buried in it. Kids die! I remember her mom screaming while running down the road, pulling her hair, frantically voicing that her baby was gone. I watched her and cried with her. We questioned why children have to die. I thought about how strange it would be to walk by my friend Marissa's house every day and know that Marissa would no longer walk out to join me.

Shortly after that horrible day Marissa's funeral approached. I had never attended a funeral before, but this one was a must because she was my friend. Marissa practiced the Mormon faith. This often included a beautiful celebration when a loved one was lost. Many times funeral services would have an open coffin. I entered the church to see my friend lying in an open coffin at the front of the church. I hesitantly walked toward her, noticing her wearing a beautiful white, silk dress. Her long, curly black hair was draped angelically over her shoulders. In her hands sat a bouquet of flowers labeled, "I love you, Oma." Oma meant grandma in dutch. I stared over her in silence.

I reached in to hold her hand, so cold, so frigid, and so lifeless. I began to weep like I never had before, seeing my friend taken from this world, from my neighborhood, from my play time for the rest of my life. The worst part of the day was when Marissa's baby sister went up to the coffin and began to shake it, insisting that her big sister wake up already. Time became a new concept to me that day.

As I cried through the service, I journeyed back in time to Marissa's life, recalling her mischievous little ways. She could really make me laugh. Neither she nor I were fond of our grade five teacher's style. He often had us on detention. Sometimes detention meant holding dictionaries in our extended arms for periods of time. We felt that at least half of our sentences were based on false accusations. One day Marissa felt the need to let Mr. C know that she didn't approve of his methods of discipline. She snuck behind his chair while he was sitting at his desk, and she ruthlessly dumped an entire bottle of Elmer's glue on his head. It was a moment of spectacular performance. Marissa did exactly what I thought of doing but never had the guts to do. She received a daily sentence of solitary confinement for that sticky act. However, I managed to sneak her in a chocolate chip cookie once in a while under the radar. The best part of this story is that Mr. C was one of the only teachers that came to her funeral that day. I think he loved her even if they didn't see eye to eye. I believe he also brought a bottle of Elmer's glue with him.

After the service, we followed the funeral cars to the grave site. The sun was shining and beautiful flowers awaited at the final destination of my friend. I remember staring at the hearse. I remember feeling sick in the pit of my stomach. I hated the thought of a car that carries bodies to the place where they will be buried. The whole thing mortified me and still unsettles me today. I always say that I should rent a hearse and take my friends out in it for a beautiful drive and a picnic to try and reverse the fear that is attached to these images from my childhood. Marissa's short life was now marked with a cross in a park on the side of the road in Castlegar.

This was a turning point in my life. I soon realized that I needed to encourage the best in people always, because time is unpredictable. Time on earth is short, and we are all just passing through. I don't want to be a cross on the road without the chance to be the best me I can be. This desire keeps burning in me and carries through my life even now.

As I meet people each day, I am drawn to the awareness of a different kind of cross evident in their lives. It makes me feel anxious. These are not crosses on the side of the road. These are the crosses that we carry through our lives that impact everything around us.

As children we often aren't aware of the crosses that we carry. Children are born with an innate optimism and an incredible shield of resilience. A child truly believes in the impossible and will look for good in all things. Children also have this wonderful gift of imagination that can create a new world of existence for them in an instant. They go to the place of the unbelievable. Children also have this incredible instinct to speak the truth and to question things that aren't right. They can hear a horrible story and be joyful; they can fall down and bounce back up. They can say sorry, mean it, and move on. They can forgive before an apology has been delivered. Children seem to live in a way that is "others centered" without really trying.

The world can change this childlike nature somehow. We begin to look at the world as if it owes us something. We live as if we are entitled to receive. It changes our perspective to a place of less resilience, to a place that is less imaginative, less adaptable, less forgiving, and more self-centered. In this state of heart, where is our deep gladness found? If we don't see the world's deep hunger, only our own, where does that leave us?

I like to think about my years teaching little children. An average day would always include an incident when one of the children would fall down on the playground. As soon as I made eye contact with the victim, the big crocodile tears started falling. Shortly after the tears ended, a lower lip quiver would follow. The episode would finally finish with the complete meltdown. These moments were so dramatic in the immediate time and space of their little lives. It seemed to be the end of the world as they knew it. But, as soon as I reached into my boo-boo bag, it would change. A super hero band-aid to the rescue and a hug, and the problem wasn't so big anymore. There was an immediate sense of calmness and comfort. Shortly after, the arm with the pulled down sleeve would proceed to the child's face. The big solid wipe of the messy, runny nose brought closure. Sooner versus later, that child got back in the game. There was no turning back, they were patched, loved, and moving on.

I find it so amazing how big people boo-boo's can stick around for so long that we sometimes never get back in the game. The cross becomes too big to carry and then the cross on the side of the road tells a different kind of story.

I have a little friend named Kayla and she sure has a big cross to carry for her age. Kayla is four as I write this book. I am so inspired by her strength and her character. Kayla was born with a very large congenital lymphangioma, a big word even for her. This mass of disease involves her right leg, her pelvis, and chest area. If Kayla is exposed to a virus of any kind, the lymphatic system responds and swells. This causes blockage to her bladder and bowel, as well as potential blockage to her airway. Kayla's little body is consumed by this life-threatening malformation. She has seen many "scary men in white coats," as she would put it. She has been poked with so many needles it is routine for her. She has even been air transferred to save her little life. What a realm of adversity for such a young person.

Kayla is marked with perfuse swelling in her right hip and leg as well as a "purple birth mark," as she calls it. This purple birth mark extends down most of her leg and buttock region. This discoloration clearly indicates that she is different than most children her age. Well, Kayla is very proud of her birth mark. Her mom was telling me that she took Kayla to her first ballet class a while back. Kayla was so excited to put on her ballet outfit, especially the frilly skirt. Kayla decided to sport the outfit without the tights that day, leaving her mom a little concerned about the reaction from the other kids in the class toward Kayla's purple leg.

As anticipated by Kayla's mom, Shannon, Kayla received many unwarranted stares. With very little grace required, Kayla stared each one of them into a corner right back! Kayla decided that nobody was going to make her feel less than beautiful in her ballet class. We all saw the fighter in her that moment. Go boldly Kayla! Kayla's deep hunger for a cure is a place of deep gladness for me, as she gives me strength.

Kayla reminds me every day to be grateful for the life that I have been given. She reminds me to see the potential to work around the things that could limit me and cheat me of a heroic life. Every time I see her, I chase her, pick her up, and squeeze her while she giggles nervously in my arms. Kayla and I both have fancy legs and we appreciate that about each other. Kayla is living with a disease that most of us would be terrified of, but Kayla has decided to stare it down and make her way in this world. She refuses to let the cross of her illness rob her of her best life. Go girl!

"In the midst of difficulty lies opportunity"
ALBERT EINSTEIN

My first surgery was when I was twelve years old. I had the operation at Victoria Hospital. My bed was located in the pediatric ward, because there were no beds anywhere else. My first night there I felt like I was in a scene from the movie "Gremlins." I could hear these little footsteps coming into my room and stopping under my bed. It was awkward for me, because my leg was strapped in the air because of my operation. I was pretty much stuck on my back. It would be quiet for some time, and then I would hear the footsteps again. I finally got a glimpse of this little yellow man with gigantic blond curls running to and fro. I was soon to discover that his name was Daniel. Daniel was left abandoned on the steps outside the hospital a short time before I was admitted. It was clear that Daniel lacked iron, as he appeared yellow with jaundice from lack of nutrition and health care. I think Daniel was around two years old. Well, those little footsteps became familiar sounds running in and out of my room. Daniel started out hiding under my bed to check me out for a while. It didn't take long until my time with Daniel consisted of cuddles, stories, and play time. I believe that was one of the days that I was certain that I wanted to be a mom. I wished I could have taken him home with me that day. Daniel had the saddest story, yet he smiled every minute and he made the people within the walls of the hospital his family. This adaptation seemed to come so naturally to him. He is a hero to me! Daniel cast his abandonment cross aside and grabbed onto life. I wonder how I would cope in such circumstances.

Quite a few years later, my high school sweetheart got in a terrible car accident and ended up severing his spine at the mid-back area. I was sixteen years old and had a National swimming career ahead of me. I was heading to UBC to get my degree in Human Kinetics and Physical Education. I remember I was lifeguarding at our local pool in Castlegar when my Dad called to tell me the news. My whole world was redefined that day!

Weeks later I went to Vancouver to visit him. With anxious anticipation, I walked through the halls of the spinal ward. I saw burn victims hanging from ceilings screaming in pain. Quadriplegics wheeled the hallways with halos screwed into their heads to prevent their spines from turning. Wheelchairs of all sizes and shapes were parked outside of rooms. As I glanced into the rooms on my way to visit Cyril, I saw many people lying in beds that strapped them in like a rotisserie. The beds were made to rotate a person onto their front and then onto their backs, while their heads peaked through a hole for air. The biggest shock to me was how young many of these patients were. Big crosses to carry for such young people! My heart sunk when I got to Cyril's room. I proceeded to lie on the floor to speak with him as his face was rotated down in the bed. I was speechless as I stared up into his scared and sad face. This was a very hard thing to see. I don't think I had ever thought about what really went on within the walls of those big hospitals.

Cyril was my friend, and I visited him every day while I was there. Each day I would see him relearning how to do life again. He had to relearn everything from dressing, to going to the bathroom, to getting onto a sidewalk, to driving a car, and the list goes on. I was surrounded with people so passionate to regain independence and to carry on with their lives. They would fall down and get up more in one day than I had ever witnessed in a lifetime at sixteen. They fell and they got up, they fell and they got up. The crosses they were dealt did not stop them finding a new way to get back up. I was amazed at their resilience. Their bigger challenges increased my world of gratefulness. I had a chronic pain issue with my leg, but I could still walk.

Some time later Cyril picked up a tennis racket and managed to get himself to the Nationals. Wow! I can hardly play a game of tennis with an able body, let alone try to steer a chair and hit a ball at the same time. I couldn't believe how a person could adapt to such drastic changes and flourish. Beautiful! I started to realize that change is the only permanent thing in this life, so I might as well be open to it.

Not too long after being a regular visitor in the hospital, I was a patient there once again. This time in the hospital consumed much of the next three years of my life. The only thing I really had a hard time adapting to was the food. I will never forget the story I was told about a young boy, I believe he was six or seven, who had terminal cancer. He was painting a picture in his room when his doctor proceeded through the door and asked him if he was going to be an artist when he grew up. The boy responded, "I *am* an artist!" That doctor learned something that day, or at least I did. He wasn't growing up in this lifetime, but I am certain that this little boy's cross is painted brilliantly! I hunger for that kind of strength.

I even recall my Intensive Care Unit roommate who, at the age of 17, had her skull opened up more than a dozen times. She had a malfunctioning shunt in her brain that needed constant adjustment. And here I worry about bad hair days.

I will never forget my roommate Anita who moved in one afternoon shortly after I came out of another surgery. She ripped the hospital sheets off her bed and covered her mattress in red silk sheets. She hung pictures of every cute boy she liked on her walls and decorated her locker with all of her special things. Wow, she knew how to live in style no matter where she slept. I was soon to learn that she was having a life threatening surgery on her occipital lobe in the back of her brain that would leave her dead or blind when complete. She was making the most of the moments while she could.

The roommate to the right of me just stared blankly at me morning and night in her coma state. She had suffered serious brain damage after being struck by a drunk driver. Her little boy would come in every day to talk to his mommy. He always asked when she would start to talk back. My soul was overwhelmed with pain as I was a witness to all these stories around me. I began to realize that if I ever began to feel sorry for myself, I needed to hang out with someone worse off. Gaining perspective is the key to resilience. I knew something about that little boy's deep pain as he watched his mom's life fade away. There was a hunger for justice brewing in the pit of my soul.

Months after my hospital stay I decided to coach swimming once again. This time I met another hero, and her name was Shelby. We were at the Regional Championships, and she was a solid competitor. Her fifty meter freestyle event was coming up. Shelby came to me to get psyched for her race. I noticed there was something different about her eyes. The whites of her eyes were yellow. She was uncharacteristically tired. Shelby was determined to go after her best time regardless of how she felt. She did and she won! Soon after her fight for the finish, she went into life-threatening liver failure. Shelby, her family, and I were on a plane to Edmonton shortly after, hoping to receive a liver that could save her life. Shelby never complained or gave up hope. She proceeded to rest peacefully in a coma, waiting on her life. I prayed! News arrived to the hospital that someone died in time to donate a liver to Shelby. Somehow that was good news. Someone became a cross on the road for another to live. Wow! We anxiously anticipated how her body would receive this gift. I went into her room after her painfully long operation, held her hand, and talked to her about our swimming stories and her friends back home. It had been so long since we received any signal from Shelby that she could hear us or knew what was happening to her. Suddenly, Shelby squeezed my hand! What a moment that was!

Shelby's body is still a little unpredictable with her new liver. Shelby's body didn't adjust to the new organ very well, leaving her chronically tired and feeling out of sorts. Shelby adapted and redirected her energy. She chose a career that can bring her more rest if needed. Shelby designs the most beautiful jewelry today that my girls and I proudly wear. Her gorgeous designer jewelry reminds us of a fighter.

The other revelation for me through all these stories is that I've learned that a life of significance often begins in the place of our truest pain. I believe this is because the most painful times are when we come to the end of ourselves. Our scars, or crosses, in other words, mark the place where we choose the path of resilience or the path of the forever wounded.

I find that the people that have the most influence in my life are the ones that have lived the most challenging lives. It is like they became heroes through adversity. The heroic act began with the choice to get to the other side of what seemed impossible. This victory marks a moment of greatness in their lives. It is from this greatness that significant life emerges. I believe that life's entirety consists of times when we are about to pick up a cross, times when we are carrying a cross, or times when we leave a cross behind. The crosses never go away, so we might as well choose to get stronger moving from one to the other. My hope is for all of us to believe, regardless of how we feel, that life is a gift to embrace. Even in pain, it is a rush to feel life to its fullest. Ask the tough questions and wrestle with the fears and the hurts, hopefully realizing that there is a presence far greater than we will ever know moving us forward. There is a purpose for how life plays out. We have the power to choose our best life so the cross on the side of the road marks the greatest legacy we wish to leave behind.

Have you thought about the crosses or burdens that are preventing you from living well? Do you recall a victory moment in your life where you got it right? Do you remember beating the odds or encouraging someone else to? Can we live with our crosses in a way that exudes joy and hope? Can we help carry the burden of someone else's cross? What do you want your cross to say at the end of this journey called life?

The Spelling Test

*"For strengths to really work in ways that change lives, they
need to become a thinking habit."*
JENNIFER FOX

have been a teacher for a long time, and I never really figured out why spelling tests were part of the curriculum. I find them more of a test of short term memory or anxiety management for those who depend on spell check like me. I do know people that love them and I am happy for those people.

I used to always say that spelling tests were for the parents. The tests provide a system to grade performance and provide homework. I think you get the hint that I am not a big fan of spelling tests or many other types of tests. I prefer to be resourceful versus masterful at short term memory retention. However, I do appreciate the intention behind tests. I also appreciate the need to measure growth somehow.

If there was one spelling test that I could offer young people today it would be the following list. My challenge would be for them to know each word by heart.

The Test

1. courage
2. uniqueness
3. forgiveness
4. passion
5. innovation
6. perseverance
7. love
8. discover
9. dream
10. imagine
11. hope
12. service
13. expression
14. purpose
15. acceptance
16. grace
17. intentionality
18. reflection
19. joyfulness
20. playfulness

Bonus Words: 1. character 2. gratefulness 3. resilience

I believe that if these words are written on your heart you will live the honor roll life! Study the core of their meaning and apply them uniquely to your journey. Store them in your long term memory bank, as we know how quickly we forget things we memorize the night before a test.

Angels Around Us

*"We are each of us angels with only one wing, and
we can only fly by embracing one another"*
LUCIANO DE CRESCENZO

was about to embark on my very first year of teaching at West
Point Grey Academy. I was teaching a full day kindergarten
class of eighteen children. I was in my new classroom antici-
pating the little people who would be joining me on some wonderful learning adventures. While setting up the classroom, I anticipated
it filled with energy and diversity. I had dreamed of this day.

I had a special place set up on the carpet where we could engage in
great conversation and sharing time. I had the desks in clusters around
the room with the little name tags placed on each one. I set up all my
learning centers around the room where the children could go and
explore their potential or create something unique. One of my favorites
was the Take Apart center, where I would put old clock radios or
machines for the children to take apart. Often children wonder what
is on the inside of these mysterious machines. It was like having a
Kinder Surprise in your classroom every day. It blew my mind when I
witnessed a boy who was able to put a machine all back together in

working order later that year. Engineer in progress?

As I was finalizing my arrangements for my first year of teaching, I heard a bit of a ruckus in the hallway. Shortly after, this handsome young couple entered my classroom, smiling and looking excited and fresh. But, soon to follow them was this screaming child. He screeched his voice like a race car as he rounded the corner into the classroom. He proceeded to investigate everything in the classroom while making the most peculiar sound effects. I thought to myself immediately, please Lord let them be in the wrong classroom. Nice, right?

I carried on a very pleasant conversation with this little boy's parents. They were funny and engaged in a very supportive conversation about the school year ahead. They expressed how their son was excited to be coming to this school. As I listened, I watched the little monkey out of the corner of my eye, realizing that I would have to put my classroom management skills to work with this little prize!

It turned out that after a few short days the little monkey worked his way right into my heart. He was so curious about everything; he would even put his hand up to say something before I could get out the question. He didn't have much control over his physical body or his verbal outbursts, but he had a sensitive kindness about him that just drew you right in. He was so full of the passion to learn that he struggled every moment to contain himself.

Tanner and I grew closer and closer as the year went on and we even hung out together outside of school. There was never a dull moment in his company. He taught me more about insects and animals than I ever could have researched on my own. Swimming lessons were also part of Tanner's and my time together at school. There was an indoor pool on the campus. Tanner was usually the first one on deck. Often we found him pacing the sides, anxious to begin the fun. In the lessons, Tanner would time and again catch me by surprise by jumping on my back or splashing a tidal wave of water in my face. Before I could lose my patience with him, he would wrap his arms around my neck and give me a huge hug. This child was addicting in a strange sort of way. He always had a bit of shock value to share that made each day a surprise.

Nothing ever went unnoticed in the company of Tanner. He was never too intimidated to ask questions or blurt out his thoughts. As I was teaching him swimming, he noticed the big, long scar down the back of my leg. Tanner said, "Mrs. Delcourt, that is the biggest zipper I have ever seen, what is wrong with you?" After I had a good laugh I started with my shark attack story, but he wasn't buying that one. So I proceeded to tell Tanner that I have a big, huge snake of weird blood vessels that grow on my nerves from my lower back down my leg. The doctors tried to take them out because they hurt. He then asked, "Did it work?" I told him that I was so special that no one could figure me out! He laughed at that one and proceeded to tell me that not many people could figure him out either. We had something else in common after that conversation.

This story didn't settle well with Tanner, because he was an answer man. So he went over to his mom and told her I had a really big owie, and she and I had a lengthy conversation about the whole deal.

I even went as far as to tell Tanner's mom that one of my motivations to become a teacher was that I wasn't sure if I could safely have children of my own, so I thought it would be great to be a day mom to a whole bunch of children. Later on that year, after more wonderful memories and many great conversations, I had quite a special relationship with Tanner's family. I was working late one night in my classroom when Tanner's dad came into the classroom with an excited look on his face. We began to chat and he proceeded to pull out four envelopes from his jacket pocket.

It turned out that Tanner's grandpa was a prominent donor to the Scottsdale Mayo Clinic in Arizona (a diagnostic clinic for rare disorders). Later I learned that Milan, Tanner's grandpa, is a donor for every hospital I have been in. What a generous spirit! The family knew that I had some serious health problems, thanks to Tanner. They also heard about my cousin's wife, who was very ill, through some stories that I shared over dinner. So Tanner's dad, Rick, said that the family insisted I go to this clinic to see the best doctors in the world. Maybe there was something they could do for my condition. To ensure that I would accept this precious gift, Rick went on further to say that they wouldn't send my cousin for help unless I went with her. They insisted that our husbands go as well. Every part of me broke down that day. I cried, and I laughed, and I screamed, and I hugged Rick speechless.

Here I thought that this little boy Tanner was going to be a little devil to reckon with. He turned out to be an angel that changed my life forever. Tanner's family holds a special place in my heart evermore! I still see them on a regular basis in a posture of gratitude! I love to tell this story because I believe it is a rarity to receive such a special gift in this lifetime. This was one example of giving big. I want a heart like that.

In case you were curious about the outcome, I received some answers and was given the safe go ahead to have children. My oldest daughter Hannah was born one year later.

I wonder how often I assume things about people from the way they may look, act or speak. I wonder how many times I give up on people that don't cater to my "feel good" state. I am learning to pray about my assumptions, because I am certain life holds the greatest treasures if we can get past our assumptions.

Experiential Learning

*"If I had asked people what they wanted, they
would have said a faster horse."*
HENRY FORD

eginning the school year with a bang was a necessity. It was important to me to offer something at school that got children to jump out of bed to come in the morning. There are so many interesting aspects about machines that fascinate young people. My teaching partner suggested that machines would really be a great study to hook the children into an excitable learning mindset. There was nothing more beneficial than to grab the children's curiosities right out of the gate. So the study of machines was where it all began.

I was amazed at how this learning process played out once the machine unit started. Studying a topic with such a broad knowledge base can often be quite an escapade. It is not always predictable. We set it up so the classroom had many different simple machines to explore; these machines included household machines that the children would be familiar with.

Every child investigated different aspects of the machines. Some of the children started and ended with the on and off switch. Others were interested in the machine parts that were removable or transformable. I even had a little boy named Jared who was a very calculated individual. He had to do the math before he even began to explore a simple machine. He dove right into the concepts of force, lift, torque, friction, etc. before he even attempted to put the machines to use.

Then there were Demi and Mitchell, who attempted to make a teeter totter with a plank and fulcrum to see if they could catapult classroom objects across the room. They figured out quite quickly that the fulcrum needed to be positioned strategically and quite a force had to be applied at one end of the plank to traject the object the farthest.

Then there was Steven, otherwise known as our "Gentle Giant." He was so proud to be tall and strong in kindergarten. When Steven heard that we were going to spend some time exploring machines, his eyes lit up like magic. Steven's dad was a carpenter and was well known for his skilled craftsmanship. According to Steven, his dad used the neatest tools to create things. When we introduced some of our interesting machines at carpet time, Steven had his hand in the air and was just bursting to share his thoughts. When I called on him, he asked if he could bring his dad to the classroom to make something with all the children. There was quite a response from the crowd at this request.

Then suddenly Hannah was inspired and put her hand up as well, wanting to bring her dad, the chemist, to class to share his tools and experiments with us. Once again, there was another wonderful response from the crowd. I ran these parent visit ideas by my teaching partner. We both agreed that it would add to the experience powerfully. It would also bring some of our community together to enjoy a hands-on experience with one another.

Within one week of this circle time, Steven's dad and Hannah's dad were scheduled in to join the wonderful world of kindergarten. Steven and his dad decided that their project would be to help all the children build cedar bird houses from scratch. They collected all the cedar and created a template for the children to follow. The coolest part was that

Steven's dad made sure there were enough supervisors to enable each child to use real machines and tools like a saw, files, a hammer and nails, etc. Wow, most children this age can barely use butter knives; this was powerful stuff! The smell in the classroom of fresh cut cedar was beautiful. The room was filled with busy hands, busy minds, and a whole lot of noise, but an incredible picture of people working together to create. I stood back and watched the children, who had smiles on their faces and wood chips scattered in their hair. They were actively participating in building something that to them was bigger than life. Their confidence grew in leaps and bounds that day and there was no way that I could have accomplished that on my own as their teacher. I think I was on to something with this parent participation. It is amazing what results from many hands working together.

Hannah's dad arrived in the classroom after the bird house project was successfully completed. He sported a fancy lab coat and carried a mysterious tool box filled with funky, clinking bottles of liquid nitrogen and all sorts of lab gadgets. He let a little liquid nitrogen fill the air like smoke with his grand entrance. The children were instantly spellbound. He began sharing the experience of using lab machines by taking a huge purple head of cabbage and freezing it with liquid nitrogen. The children gazed on. He then proceeded to take a pick-like tool out of his box to shatter the purple cabbage into pieces. Who would have known that purple cabbage could shatter? He transformed things from solids, to liquids, to gas in front of their very eyes. Fascinating stuff! I don't think my room had ever been that quiet. Once the show was over, he let the children dive into the chemistry of his tool box. There were phrases like "presto," "shazam," and even "shishboomba" murmured around the room. The children felt like magicians transforming all these items into different states of matter and more. The day just disappeared, and I hardly felt like I worked one minute.

We soon discovered that this momentum became contagious. The head master of our school had a son, Patrick, who was considering medical school. Patrick often visited and brought us coffee or treats to the staff room on his days off. Everybody loved Patrick. He seemed to visit the primary wing quite a bit. The little people are purely entertaining. When he learned that we were studying machines in science, he suggested bringing in some cow hearts to dissect with the children. He was certain that the children would love to learn how their hearts worked. Doctor machines are also pretty handy. I hesitated for one second about the potential gory scene that could happen among my five and six-year-olds. We decided to talk about the option with the children and to vote on the subject. When we asked the children if they wanted to become heart surgeons, they all screamed with disgust and then shook with a bit of anxious anticipation. Shortly after the drama, the children yelled, "Yah!" The vote was unanimous, so the show went on.

You see, at the age of five or six, most children visualize a heart like a valentine that is perfectly shaped, in hues of pink, red and purple. I really don't think that they anticipated a bloody, fleshy, ball of tissue with masses of muscles, tendons, arteries, veins, and valves holding it together.

The day arrived when Patrick was coming to the class with his cow hearts and machines to share with all the children. We had all the surgeons dressed in lab coats. I was draped in my Mad Scientist attire with gloves and sanitary wipes on hand. Each group of four children had a dissecting tray and the machines to explore the organ. The one mystery item that was on the tray was a straw. What would a straw possibly be used for unless we were going to drink the blood? Only Tanner, Khalid, Mitchell, DJ, Malcom, Lauren, or Demi would say that to freak the whole class out for fun.

The journey began with Patrick taking a heart out of a plastic bag. He held the heart in his open hand for all terrified eyes to look upon. I sat back and watched the smorgasbord of frantic expressions that first responded to the visual. As Patrick began to talk about the heart and its amazing function within the body, there was an ease that set over the children. A natural curiosity was sparked. The children moved in closer, some tempted to feel, others smelled, and some still held back with a grimace all over their faces. This was the beginning of facing their fears, of moving over the barrier to the other side. Would they survive?

Patrick cut the heart with a scalpel. This was to expose the four chambers on the inside of the heart. He proceeded to explain how blood flows in and out through the valves in order to keep the heart pumping. Then Patrick picked up the straw from the tray and proceeded to put it into one of the valves of the heart. The children held their breath. He positioned the straw into a valve. He then put his mouth over the open end of the straw and began to blow into the heart. The heart began to expand like a balloon. Screaming was the only sound coming from my classroom at that very moment. But, crazy enough, it became the turning point when all the children wanted to get their hands dirty to explore these incredible machines called hearts. I have never seen so much blood and fun in a room at one time! I even think I witnessed a few potential doctors emerging from the experience, possibly even a director of Thriller Films in progress.

I was amazed at what happened when the children overcame their fears, but I was suddenly developing a fear for my next parent/teacher conference. Hopefully there were no animal activists in the families. Just to clarify, all those cows died of natural causes.

Honestly, this was the time when I truly realized that children have the fearless capacity to pioneer their way through life and to learn as much as they possibly can. The best part of the learning journey that keeps me motivated as a teacher is the privilege to facilitate the "ah ha" moment. The opportunity to see the light bulb go on. The expression of discovery is a beautiful picture!

There is always something new under the sun. I hope we never forget that. Beautiful! Young people are learning machines! They are ready and willing to go above and beyond if we will let them go. I encourage all parents, teachers, coaches, and peers to foster one another in the lifelong learning process. Continue to navigate your thoughts, questions, dreams, and doubts, so that you can experience abundant life.

The journey to discovery is the path that makes your life your own and not someone else's.

I hope that I can remain open to the learning energy in the world around me. I wonder how many fascinating experiences I have missed because I put my questions aside or I thought that my curiosity was trivial. I encourage us all to foster the process of learning, crave to seek our own truth, and enjoy the "ah ha" moments!

Attesters and Informants

*"The human voice can never reach the distance that
is covered by the still, small voice of conscience."*
MAHATMA GANDHI

o attest to something is to bear witness to something, to affirm its correctness, and to clarify its official capacity. To be an inform- ant is to supply people existing inside a closed system with infor- mation that exists outside that system. Therefore, my conclusions are that every single soul is an attester and an informant in this world. The reason we are these is because we need to make sense of the world in which we live. We attain an innate desire to understand the world around us. We also attain an innate desire to live a life marked with meaning and purpose. The risk to this innate wiring is the default per- sonality that will assume things about the world around us if we can't understand it. Often when we can't understand something, we tend to fear it or justify its existence to meet our comfort level. Who doesn't want to be comfortable?

What do you think of when you hear the term labeling? Many of us like labels, because they help define things for us. Others may refer to labels as limitations. The irony of labels, outside of the fact that they may help define, is that they have the debilitating ability to inform us of what exists within the "inside system." A label serves to narrow our vision. This narrowing vision is confirmed by knowing what things are from the label rather than what they have the potential to become.

Labeling has an incredible power to shape our environment and the experiences around us. It also has an incredible impact on the thing or person being labeled. The problem with limiting vision is that we stifle the opportunity to build, adapt, change, and grow. The Hebrew word for constructing and building is "asah," which implies an ongoing process. I would like to refer to all of us as "asahs," or "great builders."

As a parent, mom, and a teacher, I have watched and listened to how the informants and the attesters create the world around them. It is such a calculated process that enables people to find their place within the world or the system. It always amazes me to see the power that some people have when establishing these labels. We have all heard some of the cultural labels used ever so thoughtlessly throughout our days. These words include labels such as "workaholic," "drama queen," "jock," "born again Christian," "nerd," "freak," "dumb blond," and the list goes on. I am sure as you read through this very short list of words, certain images or people automatically come to mind. I am sure that we even share some of the same thoughts, even if we don't know each other, because these stigmas are so engrained in our culture. The angry kid that picks on people is the "bully." Then there are the "queen bees" and the "wannabes," that make up the rest of the world. Don't be shocked if these terms ring true to you now, because they have incredible power to penetrate the generations.

This reminds me of some wisdom that my friend Werner shared with me. He began by asking me a simple question, but one that held incredible merit with me. He asked me if it was important for me to make people happy or to please people. I told him that it has been central to my ambitions in the past, but not so much now. He said, "If everybody is your friend, you stand for nothing." There is much truth to that, because there is no way that life will not meet resistance along the road of relationships. If we stand for some powerful values in our lives, we are certain to offend some people. This led me to ask myself if I would rather follow a crowd and stand for nothing or lead and stand for something but possibly be alone. That is a tough call in life, as it is more fun to be popular sometimes.

As I mentioned before, we often limit ourselves by labeling things simply because we don't understand them. We fear what we may discover if we explore further. This is especially true when we label people. It is impossible to capture the entire essence of an extremely complex human being. Each person is a symbol of mystery and uniqueness. How could we ever possibly know or fully appreciate a human soul? They are free thinking, changing, persevering machines that have a universe within themselves that only God himself could ever understand. My dream is that people will intentionally seek out how others are different and then celebrate their differences. Diversity can create a beautiful synergy, because it models new ways of knowing, being, and thinking in the world. It is the hope for a better future.

I have used many labels throughout my life. I am still working on the awareness of that language and how it can impact my experiences. I am especially good at identifying the bully in the crowd because I had a great deal of first hand experience with these stereotypical behaviors as a young teenager. My unique personality was a magnet for bullies.

I recall many days phoning my big brother Darren at school to bring his girlfriend and her sisters to meet me after school so I could make it home alive; at least it really felt like that. I received many phone threats that a gang of girls would be waiting for me after school. I had girls write me letters to tell me all the reasons why I didn't fit in. Sometimes it was because of the clothes I wore or the choices I made. It seemed like nothing I did met the grade in their eyes. I didn't really enjoy my high school years for this very reason. I intentionally got involved in activities outside of school, so that I had a chance to make friends in other circles. The circles were quite connected because I was from a pretty small town. In grade eleven I took the first opportunity to leave Castlegar when a swimming scout suggested I try winter swimming. There was no indoor pool in Castlegar, so I had to move to be able to try this experience. Near the end of grade eleven, I made my way to Vernon to live with a family and to explore the world of competitive swimming a little further.

I had a great experience in this community. I had the chance to experience some healthy friendships in Vernon. Thank goodness, because for a while I thought there was something seriously wrong with me.

As I grew up and grew more confident, I ran into one of these bullies from my home town while at University. I crossed paths with her in the bathroom at a dance on campus. I wasn't sure if I should hide in my stall or come out. I came out on a hope and a prayer. I said hello and then cut to the chase and asked why she was such a bully in high school. She received my boldness quite graciously. Without hesitation she replied, "I was jealous of your life." Wow, nothing like coming clean. I did have a pretty good life. I had an awesome family that supported me and two big brothers that looked out for me. It turns out that her life wasn't so great. She was sad inside and chose me to lash out at in high school. I wish I had known then what I know now, because I would have responded differently. I learned that I often respond to how people make me feel. Bad feelings warranted bad relationships for me. The humbling insight I discovered was that responding to people based on how they make me feel just turns the focus right back on me. Then we start to become attesters of other's lives, leaving a label that grows to a place of possibly no return. The label I gave to that bully ended in that bathroom and I left with a new understanding and a different way to "see" a bully. I noticed that the labeling ended with the understanding. Interesting!

It wasn't until my daughters reached grade school that this tolerance in me for bullying was tested. It is amazing what happens in a mom when her baby gets picked on at school. I believe that all realms of reason, emotional intelligence, and self-control disappear completely and the mother bear is birthed for all to see.

My oldest daughter Hannah turned ten and was entering the world of grade five girls. She was experiencing all the stuff that goes along with it: popularity, choices, body changes and all that jazz. She was being bullied by this one girl at school. Hannah often came home crying and pleading with me, not wanting to go back to school. My husband and I reflectively listened to the patterns of this relationship. We took some deep breaths, prayed, and came up with a game plan to deal with this girl. It started with inviting the bully over to our home for lunch. We felt that most often bullies just want your attention, so we thought it best to give this one some healthy attention. We did lunch, but the problem didn't really improve. The famous wisdom of "use your words," was the next strategy, but we were soon to learn that it was doomed for failure. Then Hannah decided to write a note to her teacher requesting help and mentorship for herself and the bully. This strategy resulted, once again, with no real success. Her final course of action was to inform the principal about her struggle. After the principal was notified, some boundaries were put in place. It is amazing how someone can abuse you from a distance with using no words at all. Well, mother bear was in full fledge "heated" stage, seeing the effort and the courage of my daughter get beaten out of her as she tried to make sense of it all. I came up with a brilliant plan. I told Hannah to just plow her; yes, there are labels for mom's like me! It felt so good to get off my chest! The sobering moment came shortly after when Hannah said, "Mom, then she has something on me!" There was a beautiful silence and a real humbling moment after that. Hannah's social entrepreneuring way saw the bully for what she was and still kept trying to break through. I am so proud of that girl; I can call her an asah, a builder of great relationships.

Fancy eyes is a title or a label that my friend Logan and my daughter Hannah can live with. This label intends to build the spirit rather than weaken it. Fancy eyes is a better name for a condition known as

Irlen Syndrome, discovered by Helen Irlen in 1980 It seems that any out of the box diagnosis is a syndrome these days. Anyway, Irlen's affects close to 26% of the population.[4] Irlen's is caused by eye sensitivity to light and it can manifest itself in various extremes within individual children. Some people report few symptoms outside of the mild ones of discomfort and fatigue. They may take longer to complete tasks of reading, writing, and math activities. Some cases can be more extreme where the child is often mislabeled as having Attention Deficit Disorder, Attention Deficit Hyperactivity Disorder, or dyslexia. Having this syndrome is not a matter of intelligence or learning styles, it is how the eyes function under certain light. There are methods that a child can use while reading to provide comfort, which results in improvement of symptoms.

When we label children or people in general, it defines their future for them. The act of labeling hinders the hope of a better life. Labeling ends the celebration of uniqueness and focuses on weakness based living instead of strength based living. It is the beginning of the death of the ageless spirit within us all.

I wonder how many people I have labeled. Maybe we should do less informing and more building. Does anyone come to your mind when we speak about bad feelings? I encourage all of us to choose to see the good in others no matter how they make us feel. I have discovered that there are many treasures in the jars of clay since I decided to change my ways.

The Hero Within

"I think of a hero as someone who understands
the degree of responsibility that comes with freedom."
BOB DYLAN

t is almost like the superhero calling in life is innate in us as
children. If we patiently watch children at play, they live out
their belief of life with a heroic style and a heroic passion. It
seems that something changes in all of us when in the company of a
child. Perhaps it is because a piece of us identifies with that sort of living—heroic living.

Lucas was a victim of my very first year teaching. I really knew
nothing about teaching my first year, but I seemed to have everyone
fooled. I have to thank all my co-workers as they modeled fabulous
style and process to make teaching an art. The school I was teaching at
had a system in place where uniforms were mandatory. When the children arrived to school in the morning the routine was to meet and greet
the head master at the door with a postured hand shake and eye contact. Once the greeting was accepted the children made their way to
their various classrooms. I wasn't always sure if Lucas would get through
the doors, as mornings were not always his best and he often arrived at

school half asleep. Almost every morning Lucas maneuvered his way to the classroom and closed the door behind him. Then, he would look over his shoulder wearing a small smirk on his face, as he proceeded to unbutton the stuffy uniform collar to reveal the red silks. Yes, Lucas was truly a Spiderman agent of his time. Uniform or not, he refused to step down from his actual identity. The uniform was the disguise to protect the hero within. He only revealed himself to those that believed! He was safe in the world of kindergarten. Kindergarten had a sacred inner circle of trust. I am sure he would have conducted an experiment on creating the new and improved Web Blaster if I would have allowed him. What a guy! I think he is in the field of science or engineering today. I hope he still sports the red silks.

Have you ever been to a children's Halloween party? Now that is something to see in this lifetime. It is the most incredible vision of transformation right before your eyes. These children have vast, adventurous imaginations that make them become the character they are dressed as. The princesses parade around, sit to tea, and dance like they live in castles among cotton candy clouds. The knights pull out their swords to slay dragons and save the kingdom. The police officers patrol the grounds looking for anyone conducting themselves in an inappropriate manor and they cuff the one out of line immediately. The animals crawl around, lick their paws, and suddenly stop speaking English and can translate cat talk. It is truly amazing! The imagination is the place where heroes are born, but the world is the place where they need to be nurtured and many times, that is where they die.

I have to admit, a family tradition was birthed from this heroic spirit that I witnessed so often in Kindergarten. This mentality of transformation and dreaming is truly contagious. Since teaching these brilliant young children, I have a tradition that I carry on to this day. I wear my wedding dress on every anniversary I celebrate with my husband Grant. I wake up extra early and put on the dress and cook him bacon and eggs for breakfast so he can be served by a Goddess. Yes, this has been going on for almost twenty years. I plan to put it on for fifty more years. The amazing thing about this day every year is that when I step into that dress I feel like a queen; I go back to the ideal of romance. I dance, sing, and spin and twirl. This tradition gets embellished every year as our two girls put on their best party dresses. Grant comes down to breakfast with a tie wrapped around his head ready to dance with his favorite girls. The dress has even made it beyond the house. It has been parasailing over Kelowna. It has been at princess parties as the fairy godmother. It has been worn to a vow renewal on the beach for our 13th anniversary. We giggle, eat, and play together, and it all started with the transformation of a dress. The bonus is I can actually still get into it.

The other plus of the dress tradition is for my hubby. He gets so excited that the "cost per wear" goes down with each anniversary, making my dress cost $52.63 to date. I don't know if I mentioned that my husband is a truly heroic chartered accountant.

My youngest daughter Madison has always dreamed of being a singer and a performer. It all started one day when my husband Grant was outside washing his car and heard a melody belting out from above. Startled by the interesting tones and pitches, he stopped washing his car to take a look around. Not only did he notice neighbors looking on and smirking, but he also noticed Madison in the second floor window of her bedroom. She was singing a song from the depth of her heart and soul. She made up a song titled, "Kiss that Cross." Her first audience was any audience she could gather from her little world. Today it happened to be the people in the neighorhood. She worked the crowd all right! We all got a charge out of her intentional performance and her bravery. She never even asked how the show went, because she was a star, and that's all that mattered at the ripe old age of seven. That's courage to be admired!

Madison came home from school one day and said, "Mom, I was a hero today." I responded, "Good for you, tell me about it." She proceeded to tell me that there was a boy with special needs at school that was getting picked on. She knew he was special because she watched him and noticed that his brain worked differently than most others. Madison's words were, "Mom, I know his brain works differently than ours so he doesn't bother me. I asked him to play with me." I think Madison is beginning to learn what heroic living is about.

I believe we all know something about heroic living; we just have to believe it can be a reality in our lives regardless of our circumstances. Children naturally seek the best in life, are game for anything, and love to dream big dreams. We were all children once and know that passion and spirit. We have to try and be active in creating a culture that keeps this spirit alive in all of us. Think of yourselves as heroes of the future. I want to be a part of that future that could otherwise be known as heaven on earth.

Alive Moment by Moment

"Don't count the days, make the days count!"
MUHAMMAD ALI

When teaching, the most challenging times of the day were the times when I had to stop an activity midstream. I had to switch gears with the children to get them to the next activity or class. Have you ever successfully tried to get a child to transition to a new activity joyfully when they are totally immersed in building something and creating? It is practically impossible without some sort of resistance being evident. Think about it, have you ever been in a sweet spot where your thoughts are flowing and you are really gaining momentum in your moment, in your passion, in your hobby, when someone completely interrupts the flow and the rhythm that you were on? Did you like it? How did you respond? I am certain that you didn't receive it well. We often forget that we do this to our children when we interrupt them in the middle of something with, "Quick, we have to get to soccer practice!"

I remember a young girl named Demi in my Kindergarten class. Demi never really gave you much to go on. She walked to her own beat. Demi's face rarely changed expression and she was very quiet most of the time. Demi's posture may portray a lack of interest, but this girl was taking it all in. She intrigued me. She didn't really live out loud, but I knew that much was happening in her little mind. One day I discovered that whenever Demi did work on paper, she wore a little crooked grin on her face and her eyes rarely lifted from the page. She wasn't distracted by random outbursts or regular classroom activity, she was just totally engaged. Demi most often handed her work in close to the end of the time allotted. I realized when I reviewed her work where Demi's sweet spot was. Demi decorated her work with the most unique and brilliantly colored designs. Her written name was designed differently almost daily. Her drawings were intricately detailed with shape and line that most kindergarten children didn't display. Demi, my little artist, came alive on paper. Every moment she had to create something from nothing on paper was when Demi was most alive. I actually saw her at a wedding two summers ago, and she is going after a future in graphic design. Surprise!

Do you ever notice what children notice? One day I was in the mall with my girls, and Madison noticed a lady and she asked me, "Why does that lady have such sad eyes, Mommy?" They are so tuned in and focused on every little detail of their immediate universe. They are truly alive in every moment. I remember when Hannah was two, and she would go for a walk with her daddy. Those walks took forever. Hannah had to squat down to examine every leaf, every bug, and every flower on the walk and tell her daddy how beautiful they were. She would examine everything so intensely and reach out to touch it and try to smell it and experience it to its absolute fullest potential.

Recently, my girls and my husband surprised me with a trip to Mexico after a difficult time with my family. Before they sent me off to the sun and beaches, Madison and Hannah reminded me of my dream to ride dolphins. Their last words to me were, "When you ride the dolphins, mom, ride them like you mean it." Really, is there any other way to ride them? Children naturally do everything like they mean it as long as their passions and interests are engaged and as long as they feel value in the experience. Imagine life lived like this every day; what an incredible experience!

After church one Sunday we were running a few errands in town. One of our favorite stops is a store called Winners. It is one of those "everything" stores that has great discounts on name brand items. It always feels good to score a cool pair of shoes or some fun clothes up to 75% off. We were driving into the Winners' parking lot when the girls noticed this man opening a can of beans on the sidewalk outside of the store. He looked a little weathered, a little lonely, but his eyes were the brightest blue ever. He looked at us with an expression that seemed to resonate with the girls immediately. Hannah said, "Mom, we should get him a hot cup of coffee." The girls continued to ask random questions about this man's state of life. They were consumed by his circumstance. The entire world disappeared around them. Once we shared some coffee with him, the intent of our stop in the shopping center took an interesting turn. The girls frantically insisted that we go home and take a stack of blankets, healthy food, clothes, etc. to bring back to this blue eyed man. Grant and I went along with this and made our way home. The girls relentlessly took blankets, pillows, and anything that they could find that would be of use to this man, and they jumped back in the car waiting to return to the center. We made our way back to Winners' only to find him gone. Both the girls were so sobered by this that they insisted that we drive all over Kelowna to find him. After an hour of unsuccessful searching, we asked the girls why they were so passionate about this. We have many poor and homeless people in our community. This case was different for them somehow. Hannah said, "He is different than the rest, mom, there was something in his eyes." Madison said, "Mommy, I think he makes good choices with his life, but something happened to him." I was amazed at their insight, and I often ask them what they "see" in many circumstances of our lives. Children feel the moments and pay attention to things that many of us adults overlook. It seems like they have a sixth sense or something. I think that sense is lost when the pace of life speeds up.

There is a song by a band called Starfield. The song is titled, "Alive in This Moment." I listen to this song often. It encompasses the journey of our lives, as the words portray a child who goes running to his or her secret place where they belong. The child just goes running to it, they don't hesitate, question, or deviate from the place where he or she belongs.

Where is your secret place? Where is it where there is nothing left to hide? Where is the place where our life is most alive in every moment, where our strengths peak, and the world is different because of it? Reach for this place, look for it, reflect on it, listen to it, and chase after it so you can live it with a vengeance! Yahhhh!

Leave Your Mark

> *"You gain strength, courage, and confidence by every experience in which you really stop to look fear in the face. You must do the thing which you think you cannot do!"*
> ELEANOR ROOSEVELT

One of my many favorite things about little children is their art creations. The best works are the pictures that are filled with lumpy potato people decorated with big goofy smiles, huge eyes, and outward reaching stick arms. I love the boldness children have to cover their work with brilliant colors. They don't fear going outside the lines. I always see kid art as a perfect portrait of a broken world with so much beauty in it.

Do you recall the many times in preschool and elementary school when you had to trace your hand and cut it out or press it into clay to mold it and paint it? Do you remember how important it was to press that hand just perfectly to make your mark? Often the print was painted and maybe even decorated with sparkles to give to mom and dad. It was the gift we were most proud of. There is not one like it! There is no other print like yours; it is a wonder all on its own. Could you imagine if we still put our handprint in the things that mattered to God and to our heart's desires? What beautiful creations we would all make!

Speaking of leaving a mark, there is one other little hero in my life and his name is Zach. Zach came into my life about six years ago when I offered backyard private swimming lessons in the summer. Zach proved to be a talented little fish and a bit competitive too. This toughness in Zach turned out to be very helpful a few years later. Zach was experiencing very uncomfortable pain in his legs. He was taken by surprise with the mysterious broken bones and found himself heading to Vancouver General Hospital to learn more about his ailments. Zach was soon diagnosed with a condition known as Fibrous Dysplasia. Fibrous Dysplasia is a disease that causes thinning of the bones. It causes growths of tissue to form in the bones and results in bone weakness and scar formation within the bones. Fibrous dysplasia is very rare, not much is known about it, and there is no known cure.

Zach has embraced his circumstances and has proven that he has the ability to adapt to create a joyful life regardless of his painful condition. When he can't participate in the bike rally, he takes photos for the yearbook. He may not be able to stand and ski, but he can sit and ski down the hill twice as fast. He can still kick butt in the pool. Zach is making his mark! He is leaving his handprint on the path of resilience daily. Way to go Zach!

The handprint imagery takes me back to the genius of Robert Fulghum's book titled *All I Really Needed to Know I Learned in Kindergarten*. It holds great value for me. I have to say that five-year-olds have provided some of the most fascinating examples of wisdom I know; in fact, if I was to ask all of you today if you were smarter than a kindergartener, we would hope so. Maybe we are smarter with generic facts and academics, but I don't think we are when it comes to pure faith and free spirit! Sure, we may know better the ways of the world, but certainly not the ways of the heart. These little people put their fingerprints on absolutely everything. Remember how to live like that! Leave marks all over the place, the ones that reflect the best you that you can be.

Stay Connected to Your Child

"Do small things with great love."
MOTHER THERESA

t is easy to forget that there is more to life than activities and responsibilities. As the pace of life continues to speed up, it is more difficult to make time to connect with the ones we love. This time is critical for us to be able to establish credible relationships with our children and family members. For children to steer their lives to be the hope for the future, the voices that they know and trust must invest in good, honest conversations with them. Time with our children must be a non-negotiable part of the day's schedule.

1. Play "I love you because…" Take turns finishing this sentence with your family members and be reminded of how much you are loved.
2. Choose a valued personal statement to share with your child like, "I trust you," "I believe in you…" "You are so important to me!" "I love you to infinity and beyond."

3. Ask your child what they think about. Cover the table with a huge sheet of blank paper and write your dreams and draw pictures of inspiration together. Create and think out loud.

4. Have a "special person" plate in your home for the members of the family that live to choose joy and make a difference somehow. Celebrate a family member by giving them the plate to eat from. Celebrate the small successes and the others centered way of living.

5. Create a family mission statement together. One of my family's statements is, "Choose joy and make someone's day!"

6. Play two stars and a wish. This is family goal setting. The two stars are the two things that you are doing well at. The wish is the goal to work on together. Open the floor to speak into each other's life with encouragement, truth, and love. Be prepared to hear truth and appreciate it.

7. Have a family hand signal or silent sign that says, "We are in this journey together."

8. Laugh out loud and have a backwards day when dessert is eaten first.

9. Celebrate the differences in one another, and build on the community within each other.

10. Always seek your child's opinion on family matters. They will surprise you. Children need to feel valued in real life circumstances.

11. Ask your child to evaluate how you're doing on the parenting end of things.

12. Go for ice cream in your pajamas.

13. Celebrate a birthday for a whole month.

14. Pray together, holding hands.

15. Eat together around the table at least once a day, and allow each person to choose the topic of conversation.

16. Spend one-on-one time with your child, and just listen to their life.

17. Slow down, pay attention, seek out the strengths in your child, and encourage them to live in them.
18. Don't take your child's reactions personally, just keep building into their lives and striving to identify with their uniqueness and enjoy them!

Fun Facts

> *"Life isn't measured by how many breaths we take, but
> by the moments that take our breath away."*
> ANONYMOUS

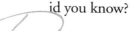id you know?

- The average child laughs three hundred times per day. The average adult laughs between ten and fifteen times per day.
- A small child possesses imaginative skill superior to that of any adult.
- A child responds full-heartedly to kissing away a hurt and to throwing away a fear because they actually believe.
- A child asks, on average, one hundred twenty-five questions per day.
- When you ask a child what makes them the happiest, you often hear responses like a butterfly, a day at the park, a piece of chocolate cake, game night with the family, dancing and singing; most adults think of more money, more time, and more energy.

- Unhappiness is the most common state of mind for adults and it doesn't make sense to a small child.

In Peterson's *The Message* he speaks about entering God's Kingdom. In Matthew 19:14-16 he writes, "One day children were brought to Jesus in hope that he would lay hands on them and pray over them."[5] The disciples discouraged this act and wanted the children to leave. Jesus interrupted the act of the disciples and proceeded to say "Let the children alone, don't prevent them from coming to me. God's kingdom is made up of people like these."[5] Further on in the book of Mark Peterson writes, "These children are at the very center of life in the kingdom. Mark this; unless you accept God's kingdom in the simplicity of a child, you'll never get in."[6] After this Jesus went to gather the little children in His arms so he could bless them.

Dare to Learn From Children

"If the facts don't fit the theory, change the facts."
ALBERT EINSTEIN

Children are like built-in radar systems in our world. The unique thing about their radar systems is that they are tuned into the things that really matter. Children pay attention to the world's state of heart. They watch everything that goes on and their ears hear it all. They process at mach speeds and have the hugest memory banks to retain information. Young people attain pioneer spirits that are fearless when it comes to free thinking and being.

My two girls, Hannah and Madison, manage to teach me almost daily. Each day brings a different experience. I love who they are and how they shape and mold my life. The best mom I can be to them is to model being a lifelong learner and to stay in touch with my ageless spirit so they can see me dream big dreams, play joyfully, and create a future of significance.

My girls remind me of joy in the simple things, like a dip in the lake at the end of the road. A simple tickle fight, dad's farm stories, mom's sucker kisses, eating ice cream on the roof of the house, snuggles, and tea with lots of talk time are a few of the simple joys we share.

The other day, resulting from my limited patience, I accused Madison of something she didn't do. She quickly made me aware of my error. I proceeded to make it right with Madi by telling her that I took back my accusation. She replied, "Mom, you can't take things back, you have to ask me for forgiveness." Ouch!

One day I was just pooped and I told my daughter Hannah that "Mom is just not going to get a whole lot done today." Hannah turned to me and said, "What more do you need to accomplish than to be the most amazing mom in the world?" I cried that day!

I remember Mitchell from my first Kindergarten class spontaneously moving to his knees to engage in a prayer right in the middle of a lesson. I listened as he asked if God would protect his mouth that day. He didn't want to say anything mean to the boy that really frustrated him. I was impressed with his boldness. He gave his worries to God and the result was rewarding. I think Mitchell was on to something.

I was baking a cake one evening to take to a dinner party with friends when I forgot that it wasn't an angel food cake, and I flipped over the pan to watch my entire cake fall to pieces. I stood still in shock that I could pull such a stunt, and Hannah's voice crept into my perspective saying, "Mom, it is a special needs cake and it always makes great trifle." Brilliant perspective Hannah, thank you for that! We laughed!

The girls decided to get creative on my birthday one year. They wanted to create something that fit my personality. The anticipated moment arrived when they handed me this mystery box. I proceeded to unwrap and open my gift to find a white pair of shorts folded in the box. I pulled out the shorts and opened them up. I soon noticed the bum of the shorts was decorated with colorful words that described me. Comfort, humor, and a whole lot of heart summed up the long and the short of my gift. Love them!

What happened to this masterful living within all of us? Maybe sometimes we tend to look outside ourselves to see what the world can bring to us, instead of looking inside ourselves to discover that we have something special to offer the world.

The world too often imposes expectations that we need to live a certain way, be a certain way, dress a certain way, and have certain things. It often pulls us into a vacuum of thinking and sensationalizes truths to deceiving levels. It becomes a race to perform somehow with the result defined for us. Pay attention to how your life teaches; make it teach something that is true to you.

Why not entertain the invisible possibility? Little children do this all the time. It is in all of us, this childlike faith that knows no boundaries. Let your life discover its soul truth and enjoy rekindling the fire of your passionate living.

Random Inspirations
from the
Childlike Spirit Within

Seek a fresh perspective.

Speak up.

Put your faith back in people!

Make up the rules as you go along because it is okay to change your mind.

Ask why until you realize that it might require a little faith.

Explore! Be Silly! Dance! Dream!

Don't save the fancy stuff for a special day.

Play fair.

Say sorry and forgive.

Say your prayers!

Love people even when they don't deserve it!

Let God surprise you.

Don't be a tattletale.

Play follow the leader and lead.

Check out new words before you use them.

Give a hug, Take a hug.

Jump in the leaves.

Get dirty and jump in puddles.

Always have a reason to celebrate someone.

Dress up for the party, and be on time.

Don't say you don't like it until you've tried it.

Sleep on the cool side of the pillow.

Have uncommon thoughts about common things to gain new perspective.

Make room for someone new.

If it smells sour it probably isn't healthy to eat.

Life is the test that you can't really study for, it must be lived.

Demand a turn.

Cheer really loud for the underdog.

Beware of people who know all the answers.

Bounce Back! Stay in the game! Patch the Owie!

Finish Strong.

Say you're sorry soon!

Little crayons leave big color!

Live Peacefully.

Nap.

Lick the spatula, and eat the dough.

If you have lost a child's attention, perhaps you're not worth listening to.

There is always someone better than you at something that you do.

Listen to your life.

Write your name like you mean it.

Bad words are impossible to unlearn.

Be the most good that you know to be, then you won't go wrong.

Share!

Speak so people understand.

Clean up your mess.

Go barefoot.

Get a happy place.

Conclusion

"If only one little unhappy child is made happy with
the love of Jesus…
will it not be worth…giving all for that."
MOTHER TERESA

child learns so much if we pay attention to them and invest in them and relate to them through the child within ourselves. Children are the hope for the future! We as adults live our best life when we pursue the cravings of our souls, to live them out passionately. Marianne Williamson wrote, "Our deepest fear is not that we are inadequate, our deepest fear is that we are powerful beyond measure. Your playing small does not serve the world. We were born to make manifest the Glory of God within us."[7] The end result of this sort of living is a life of joy and purpose! A life marked with such things automatically liberates others to live the same way.

You see, friends, there are stories all around us every day. There are stories that we need to pay attention to. There are stories that we need to engage in. There are stories that we have to tell. There is a story yet to be lived. All that is required is that we live wide awake and pay attention to the stories unfolding around us from moment to moment. In doing this your life will be grounded in meaning, purpose, and fulfillment. Your life will be rekindled with a fire of significance!

Choose joy! Dream big! Know that your life is precious and significantly transformational.

"You were called to share one hope...."[8]

EPHESIANS 4:4

Go and create your glorious future!

Endnotes

1. Eugene Peterson, *The Message* (Colorado Springs: Helmers & Howard, Publishers Inc., 1988), 19.

2. Dr. Suess, *Happy Birthday to You – Party Edition* (New York: Random House Children's Book Inc., 1987), 9.

3. Jenifer Fox, *Your Child's Strengths* (New York: Penguin Group (USA) Inc., 2008), 8.

4. Helen Irlen, *The Irlen Method*, Perceptual Development Corp., 1998, http://irlen.com.

5. Eugene Peterson, *The Message* (Colorado Springs: Helmers & Howard, Publishers Inc., 1988), 51.

6. Eugene Peterson, *The Message* (Colorado Springs: Helmers & Howard, Publishers Inc., 1988), 99.

7. Marianne Williamson, *Our Greatest Fear*, Harper Collins, 1992, http://explorersfoundation.org.

8. God's Word to the Nations Society, *Gods Word* (Florida: Green Key Books, 2003), 1036.